CHURCHBURNER

All characters in this book are fictitious, and any resemblance to actual persons, living or dead, is purely coincidental.

No part of this publication may be reproduced, stored in a retrieval system, or transmitted in any form by any means electronic, mechanical, photocopying, recording, or otherwise, without the publisher's prior consent.

Everything within this book is protected by copyright, but we of the dark covenant are outlaws and black magicians, therefore we will not rely on the law. If you fuck with us, we will fuck with you.

Copyright © Castaigne Publishing, Evan Dean Shelton, Caine Del Sol 2023

Printed in The United States of America

First Edition

Cover and interior Churchburner illustrations by Glenn Brewer.

Zathane illustration 1 by Brayden Turenne

Zathane illustration 2 by Papa Rotty

Interior Layout by Sam Richard

Castaigne
publishing

Contents

CHURCHBURNER
Evan Dean Shelton

PERETZETH - the Queen of Desire

December 23rd, 1993

The little room smelled like old books and cigarette smoke, and felt like at least three kinds of fear. The old man was on his ass on the floor, looking up at Kim while J rummaged through the desk. The old man wasn't paying any attention to the gun, he was looking right past it at what little of Kim's face he could see over the bandanna and under the hood.

"There ain't no money in there." The old man said. His weathered brown face was bunched up in worry, and swelling on one side from where Kim had knocked him good with the pistol.

"Ain't lookin' for money, preacher man." Kim said.

J pulled an old cigar box out of a drawer and put it on top of the desk next to his .357. He flipped open the lid, looked inside for about two seconds, then picked up his revolver and used it to flip the lid closed again. Something dark washed over the narrow band of his pale face that was visible between bandanna and hood.

The old man shifted on the floor, and took a hard look at the door to the little room. It stood ajar, and down a short hallway, past rows of old pine pews, he could see Jesus on the cross. Jesus was so far away, the old man couldn't tell if Jesus' eyes were on him or not. Then again, they always were, right?

"What is it?" Kim asked J.

For a while, J said nothing, then after what felt like a black oceanic forever...one word. "Pictures."

Kim took a deep breath and stepped away from the preacher, then leveled her 9mm at his head.

"Naw, let that motherfucker burn." J said.

Kim's brown eyes flashed red, and her arm shook from shoulder to wrist. She looked volcanic and goddamn *dangerous*.

The old man looked up at her from the floor, still ignoring the gun. "You gon' burn me?" He asked.

"Ima do worse than that, motherfucker!" Kim screamed and hit the old man across the face with her pistol again. A piece of the old man's face tore off and hit the wall with a tiny splat. Kim dropped the gun and pounced on him. J stepped around the desk and grabbed Kim by her arms, dragging her back from the preacher. Kim popped up from the floor and spun around on J, nailing him in the chest with both of her open palms and all her weight. J keeled over backward into the wall and stayed there, putting his hands up in a boxer's defense.

"Keep yo goddamn hands off me J." Kim said.

J didn't respond. There was only one response possible for him, and he left it at that.

The preacher was crying now, curled up on the floor and cradling the ruin of his face. "Y'all gon' kill me? Burn me up? You walkin' with this devil? This white devil!?" He moaned.

Kim stepped over and kicked the old man hard in the back. He yowled and rolled over to look up at her, instinctively curled up like a baby. Kim crouched over him, drawing in close over his bleeding face. "I knew yo old ass was stupid. You done a lot of stupid, nasty-ass shit. But I ain't realize that you can't even count."

"What?" The old man said.

"I said yo old ass must not be able to count, cuz there's mo than just one Devil in this room, motherfucker." Kim stood up and looked at J with a flat glare.

J stepped out into the hallway and came back in with a gas can. Kim took the gas can from J and poured it on the old man. The old man moved surprisingly quick, rolling over and making a mad scramble toward Kim's legs. J stepped forward and kicked the preacher in the shoulder, spinning him around and away from Kim to land on his back, where his moaning was choked off by the gasoline that Kim poured straight down his throat.

When Kim had nearly emptied the can, she slung what was left all over the tiny office. A generous heaping of gasoline splashed across the preacher's family bible where it stood on the top shelf. It was a one hundred and sixty-year-old tome, given to Reverend Tompkin's great-great grandfather by the man who had owned him. A dedication on the inside cover read: "To our dear and invaluable George. May the light of the Lord and Saviour be upon him for all his days." How quaint is the love of a captor for its captive...

"Please...please..." The preacher begged through gasps of air.

"Beg *god* please. Ask *that* motherfucker and see what happens. Did any of *them* beg?" Kim pointed at the cigar box on the desktop.

The preacher just kept crying.

"Did my sister beg?" Kim asked.

"It don't matter, Kim. Don't matter if she begged, that don't mean anything, anybody would-" J started.

"Aight, aight." Kim interrupted. "Aight. That ain't important. But I *do* want you to beg god. You better pray yo ass off, cuz I ain't never seen nobody pray so hard they could put fire out."

"Please, I got some money under the desk, please..." the preacher begged.

J grinned at Kim and started feeling around under the desk until he found a gallon ziploc bag with stacks of cash inside, duct taped to the underside of the desk. He tore it free, took a quick look at the contents, and stuffed it in his dirty, faded jacket.

"Thanks for the money, dumbass. Die slow. If there's a hell, tell 'em The Lupercalians sent you. Tell em you fucked with the wrong goddamn ones." Kim said.

Kim looked at J, and J nodded, then the two of them walked out of the little office, down the short hallway, and out of the church. On the front steps, J lit a match and dropped it just inside the front door, where the gasoline soaked carpet birthed fire from its faded red fibers, fire that reached into the dark recesses of that old church like the serpentine tongue of a dragon.

As Kim and J hustled over to the beat-up van parked in front of the church, they heard the preacher start screaming. The fire was already pouring out of the front door, belching flame into the night. J looked across the hood of the van at Kim. The fire was filling the pale corners of her dark eyes, and she looked ferocious. Scary. It made J think of when they were kids, Kim with the scissors in her hands, blood everywhere, and that look in her eyes. The look of a wild thing in a corner. Most of the time that look made him love her even more, but sometimes it made him wonder if one day she would let it loose on him too. Then everybody. Nights like those he went to sleep thinking he might wake up with a knife in his neck, but he'd be fine with that if it happened. There were worse things.

Kim saw the look on J's pale face as the fire washed over it and turned it orange. He looked cold in his ratty old jacket the color of nothing. It was a cold night, but he looked frozen. She was scaring him again. She loved him, she didn't want to scare him, ever. But there were worse things.

J opened the driver's door to the van. Kim took one last look at the church. The flames were reaching into the sky now, and it was starting to get loud. It sounded mad as hell, mean as fuck. Like that shit J made them listen to in the van. The sound of the wood roaring and rattling and screaming into the night was music.

"You hear that, J? It's like that black metal bullshit you like so goddamn much." Kim said.

J tipped his head to the side and listened for a second. "Goddamn..." He said, and his mouth hung open. The hellacious roar washed over him and he felt like his feet might come off the ground. From within the abrasive conflagration, J could hear something like a word or a name being scorched into the night, fumed from the throat of a living furnace. "*Zathane...*" J looked at Kim and saw that her eyes were open wide and her hand was creeping into her jacket where she kept her 9mm. She had heard the word too...

A voice from within the van spoke up. "It's gon' sound like the goddamn po-leese soon, y'all dumb motherfuckers! C'mon, let's go!" Big J sounded scared. He didn't get scared much, but when he did, he couldn't hide it.

Kim pulled her eyes away from the church and got into the van, slamming her door shut. J got in and turned the engine, and they got the fuck out of there.

"Put one of them tapes in, J." Kim said once they were on the highway.

J dug around between the seats for a moment and pulled one of his many hand labeled tapes off the pile, holding it up in the pale light filtering in through the van's windows. One word was written on the blank cover: BURZUM. He put the tape in the deck and cranked the icy noise that came out of the speakers until his ears hurt just a little bit, then left the dial there. Kim smiled a little. J smiled more. He thought she'd never get into that shit.

"Y'all both lost y'all's goddamn minds." Big J said from the backseat. He lit a blunt, and for a few seconds his huge scarred face was visible in the darkness, framed by his thick dreadlocks. His brow was bunched, face knotted in an iron pile of expressive muscle. He puffed the blunt a few times to get it going, inhaled deeply, and leaned back into his seat. "What y'all do in there?" He asked. His voice was hard and flat like a brick.

For a moment no one answered, there was just the noise on the stereo, noise from some dark frozen forest on the other side of the world. The forest outside the van was dark as well, and though not quite frozen, it was certainly cold as hell.

"We found some money. A good lil bit." J said, finally.

"Was anybody in there?" Big J asked.

"I killed the stupid motherfucker." Kim said.

"We killed him." J said.

Nothing but growling throat and snarling guitar and the rat-tat-tat of snare drum for a bit, then...

Big J started laughing. He leaned up and passed the blunt to Kim. "If we end up in jail ima tell 'em the Devil made me do it." Big J said.

"They'll fry yo big ass like bacon either way." J said.

"Sheeit...I ain't do nothin' to get fried!" Big J protested.

"They ain't gon' give a fuck." Kim laughed at the back of her throat like a panther, barely a hint of a smile even showing on her face. She passed the blunt to J. "And we ain't gettin' caught. Never."

They finished the blunt without speaking, filling the van with thick smoke like the breath of daemons while they listened to the Norwegian blackness that was lacerating its way out of the speakers and into the world. The Virginia woods rolled by. Kim thought about the fire. J thought about the fire in Kim's eyes. Big J thought about the fire where he stood and bled for Kim and Lil J the summer before. Where they had bled for him. The fire where he said the words and meant every one. Where he murdered fear. Where he put the mark on his skin and they put the patch on his back and told him it was forever. He remembered how bad Lil J's face had looked and he remembered feeling like shit for having done that to J, but J was smiling up at him so hard through busted lips and bloody teeth. He was *crying*, and not crying like no bitch, he was just that goddamn happy. Nobody had ever looked at Big J like that his whole life, not since his gramma died and he was on his own. That shit was love, and though Kim didn't show it much, he felt it from her too. He knew.

Big J crushed what was left of the blunt when they were finished and dropped it into a sticky, stinky pill bottle with a collection of other blunt roaches, then closed it up and stashed it in his backpack. He stretched out in the backseat and tried to find something to enjoy about the goddamn noise coming out of the stereo. This was forever, they had told each other. But they all knew forever wasn't shit.

TZELSAMON - THE SHADOW OF THE LORD

Two DAYS LATER, they were somewhere in Kentucky when they saw the news on a motel room television. The newsfolk were calling the church burning a hate crime. Which wasn't wrong, really...

Big J was having first shower (the motherfucker was hard to beat at arm wrestling) and Kim and J were making salads on the motel bed and watching the news. Kim grabbed the remote and turned up the volume when she realized what they were seeing. They had missed most of it already. There was a field reporter on site, and the church was a pile of grey rubble and ash, still puffing out thin smoke. The field reporter was just finishing saying something...

"Authorities believe this was a racially motivated crime, and say they are optimistic they will find the perpetrators. Kali ma, Sebastian." The program then cut back to the khaki colored non entity that was reading the news from behind a desk.

Kim and J shot each other a look, eyes wide.

"Did you hear that?" J asked

"She said Kali ma. On goddamn TV." Kim answered.

"We're trippin'. She ain't say that." J tossed a cherry tomato in his mouth and popped it between his teeth.

"Yeah, she did." Kim cast a glance toward the bathroom.

Big J's low rolling voice was pouring out from the crack under the bathroom door along with the steam from the shower. He was singing, "Sunny days, everybody loves them, but tell me baby can you stand the rain..." There was a shadow in the back corner of the motel room, near the bathroom door. The steam from Big J's shower was piling up at the edge of the shadow like it was made of glass, like it was an invisible surface that the steam was crawling along.

"You see that?" Kim asked J.

"What *is* that?" J said.

"*TZELSAMON...*" A voice crackled from the television like static snarled into the shape of language. The news program was gone, and the television looked like an empty hole full of fog. The fog was pouring out of the mouth of the television and spreading across the carpet toward the bed where J and Kim sat with their salad ingredients surrounding them. The smell hit Kim, and she stood up from the bed. Not fog, it was smoke. Smoke like a house fire. Like a church.

Kim stood up and spoke to the television. "There ain't no guilt here, motherfucker. Whatever you are, we ain't interested."

The smoke lolled from the maw of the television, a vaporous tongue that was slowly swelling and filling the floor. The inside of the television was the throat of black forever, a tunnel that stretched so far into the unknown distance that the tiny dagger point of cold light at the end of it looked like a star in the night sky. Somewhere down that tunnel, maybe miles or maybe meters...something moved. Kim and J both saw the shape in the tunnel, and both sank to their knees on the smoke buried carpet.

"J..." Kim croaked. The name came out strangled, stillborn.

The snarling static was filling their heads, low-boiling their brains in a black vat of violent noise, making it hard to focus.

The dark shape in the television tunnel drew closer...

"Goddamn, Kim...I can't...I can't..." J couldn't remember what he wanted to say long enough to say it. It was hard to breathe. Time was coming in choppy loops that were rolling him deeper with each repetition like undertow, burying him further and further into the black. Everything was smoke and static.

Kim heard someone talking but couldn't tell what language they were speaking. She was looking up at the smokey surface of a black ocean as she sank further into its depths. She couldn't remember how she got there, but she knew it wasn't where she wanted to be. She clawed at the black but just kept sinking. The smoke and static had already filled her head and now her lungs were filling and she was forgetting what it was like to have ever tasted clean air. *"Everything was good and then fuck so bad so quick oh fuck it's on top of me it's on top of me..."*

The box frame of the television creaked and groaned as it began to dilate. The dark shape in the tunnel was close now.

Kim and J were both thrashing in the water like drowning tigers, teeth bared and eyes peeled with the One True Fear. Crystalline growths of foul memories formed along their arms and legs and weighed them down. Dim projections played out along the gnarly angled surfaces of these crystal cancers, transmitting nightmarish olfactory reminiscences along with the visuals; trailer park foster homes mildewed with piss and predatory hunger, powdery dumpster apples that tasted like five hundred years of blood crusted iron oppression, greasy tendons pulling a pale face back in a smile, a snarl, a toothy creaking groan like the murmur of the gallows like the taut whimper of sailing ropes on a heavily laden ship, teeth teeth teeth that stand straight and white like the fences that keep out the undesirable and unrecognized, teeth teeth TEETH bared and shining and radiating pure Empire, shining like dead stars illuminating mice that squirm under the weight of a boot polished in slave sweat...

"I can't breathe. I can't breathe." The thought swallowed up both Kim and J's minds, and they disappeared into the black.

BERACHESH - THE RAVEN SAINT OF THIEVES

THE WORLD CAME BACK to Kim slowly. She felt like a rock on a shoreline, slowly being uncovered and revealed by each washing wave. The black dissolved, dried up like sea foam in the sun. The molasses of the void slowly ran out of her ears and eyes and mouth, and the chaos of air and light and sound returned like sensory acid, like sea air on forged steel. There was a deep rumbling and a rhythmic sway. She reached up and clawed at the last of the void molasses that was pouring from her throat, pulling it out like a gelatinous black worm lodged within her. She gasped.

"You alive?" She heard Big J's voice, but all she could see was blinding white gold. Big J sounded scared.

"Where...J at?" She asked.

"Right there next to you. Had to roll the fuck outta that motel. Po-leece gon' be after us soon f'sho. Probably..." Big J answered.

"What happened?" Kim managed to push herself upright in the van's backseat. Shapes were beginning to form in the light that was assaulting her eyes, but she still couldn't see properly.

"Y'all set the goddamn motel room on fire I guess, that's what happened. Then...I don't know. I don't wanna talk about it."

Kim sat in silence for a moment, then fumbled around in the seat until she found J curled up next to her. She put a hand on his heart. It was beating. She had too many questions, and her mind wasn't together enough to ask any of them. She felt like an ever expansive ocean of thought trying to cram itself into a mason jar. She felt like everything before now was a long dream and she was just waking up from it into something mysterious to her. The only thing she knew for sure was that J was alive, and that was...something.

Another hour down the road and Kim could see again, but she wished she couldn't. Big J must have known something wasn't right, but he stayed quiet and just kept driving. Kim gripped her old denim jacket in one hand and held onto J's with the other. She could see again, but nothing made sense, all just alien shapes and alarming colors. Cars roared by on the winding Kentucky highway like strange monsters plowing their way through towering unfamiliar wilderness. Kim knew the names for these things and the constituent identifying concepts, but there was another layer of her, a layer in which every-thing was...amorphous. Unknowable. The two layers were in combat for her attention, making it difficult to focus. She had been in states like this before, during Lupercalia moons when she and J had eaten more mushrooms than were necessary, ending the night laid out in some stretch of woods and watching the roots of the world take hold of them and spread them out like soil. She gripped the old denim and waited it out. The van cut its way down Highway 21, slicing through the Appalachian Mountains and the ancient emerald towers of wilderness that occulted them. There were pools of shadow here which had not been torn by light since before the name America was ever uttered.

Soon enough, J coughed himself awake and started pulling at the air in front of his teeth, his lips wrenched back and his mouth and eyes open wide. "J, it's me. I'm here." Kim said.

"I thought y'all was gon' die. Goddamn..." Big J gripped the steering wheel and rocked his hands back like he was throttling a motorcycle, his stony knuckles flashing pale for a moment.

The sun sank below the mountains, and darkness seemed to emerge from the forest like a god sized swarm of black martins taking to the sky to devour the light.

ZATHANE - THE MAW OF TIME

THEY SPENT the next night at a campground in north Georgia, but by lunchtime the following day they had moved on. Too many frightened and prying eyes launching daggers at the two black folks and one white dude with gang patches on their backs.

That evening, they were sitting in the van, eating Pizza Hut and drinking Cheerwine, when Big J finally told them what he saw in the motel room. He had finished with his pizza and was splitting a White Owl to roll an after-dinner blunt. "I know y'all gon' say you believe me, I know you will. But you ain't gonna get it. Ain't no way you can. You have to have seen it."

Kim and J just kept eating their cheeseless pizza and let him talk.

"I came out the shower and the damn TV was on fire, and y'all was on the floor on y'all's knees like...I don't know. I seen people on that fry that looked like that. I ain't know what was goin' on, but there was smoke every damn where and y'all wouldn't talk so I grabbed y'all and dragged ya lil asses outta there then went back for our shit. When I was steppin' outta there I looked back one good time to make sure I had everything, ya know? And the TV stretched out like a pussy and somethin' came out like a baby, man. I ain't fuckin' around.

It fell onto the floor. It was like a rotten pork chop the size of a dog, but as soon as it hit the floor it stood up tall as fuck like...like a woman. Some big ol' jacked diesel black bitch wearin' leather and armor and a goddamn helmet that covered her eyes, but I could see her mouth and goddamn man she was *smilin'* like the Devil. There was somethin' black drippin' outta her mouth onto her boots, and that bitch just *grinned* at me with that shit drippin' off her teeth and I was so goddamn *scared*, man. I saw it all like...in pieces, like when y'all had me on them shrooms when I patched. Shit was...I felt fucked up. I thought I wasn't gon' get outta that room, I couldn't *move!* Then she said somethin'..."

Kim and J let their eyes meet, each trying not to look as frightened as they were.

"She was talkin' through all that shit comin' outta her mouth, so it was kinda hard to understand, but she ain't say much. I got it. She said: "I will fatten you on sorrow and feed on your broken hearts. I will strip the meat of you away from the bones, little wolflings." Big J paused, staring at the blunt guts spread out all over one of J's zines like he was looking at himself disemboweled. "I ran as fast as I could."

For a moment no one spoke.

"I thought y'all said all this ritual shit was just in our heads." Big J said. He put the finishing tucks on the blunt and twisted it up.

"Hard to say, big man. I guess..." J shrugged.

Kim stuck a finger into her afro and tapped on her skull. "Everything starts in here, but shit gets out sometimes."

"You think?" J asked.

Big J sparked up while Kim and J wiped the pizza grease off their hands and mouths. Outside the van and beyond the edge of the Pizza Hut parking lot, a red Georgia river flowed by under a grey January sky. "It was real, y'all. Da fuck *was* it?" Big J leaned up from the backseat and passed the blunt forward to Kim. Kim inhaled deep and leaned back into her seat, watching the river go by. Watching her thoughts go by, a billion of them, and her just bobbing along the surface like driftwood.

"Maybe the motel is haunted." J said.

Big J laughed. "By some big black bitch that knows us?? She called us *wolflings*, motherfucker!"

Kim passed the blunt to J. "Fuck that bitch. Good thing she know a wolf when she see one."

Big J looked at the patch on Kim's back, the one they all wore. He could just see the ears and eyes of the snarling wolf, and the word LUPERCALIANS up top, across the back of her shoulders. He remembered the way Kim had looked the night he earned his patch, like a murderous goddess in the firelight with blood in her teeth and a black halo around her head. She had screamed so loud when she broke two of Big J's ribs with an elbow, he wasn't sure if it was the blow or the sheer volume of the battle cry that made him puke all over himself and go down onto one knee. J was on him quick after that, and shit got hazy for a minute...but here he was. Wearing the patch. A hungry wolf among the sheep of a crumbling empire. A shapeshifter wearing the face of man. An adversary. Sworn. But the big woman in the armor was...something else. He remembered the way the room smelled like his gramma when the big bitch had plopped out of the television like rotten meat...

"You don't understand. You can't. Not unless you seen her." Big J said.

"Maybe we will." J said, handing the blunt back to Big J.

TATHOS - THE VOICE OF THE MASTER

A DAY LATER, they were parked outside a brutalist monolith of institutional segregation, a squat block of brick the color of blood in the dirt. This red titan of architectural oppression was one of many in Herndon Homes, a housing project in Atlanta, Georgia. This place was a temple, dedicated to rage, anointed in the oil and incense of blood and dope smoke. The sidewalk and concrete pathway that ringed the temple were covered in the sigils and wards of the temple's order, the holy markings of the Herndon Homes Boys.

Big J flipped the safety off on his .380 and tucked it into his jacket. "We ain't gotta do this. There's still almost a thousand dollars from the preacher, we can keep on 'til Camilla and-"

"Ain't no money down there." Kim interrupted. "Unless we wanna deal with po-leese or them crazy-ass Mexicans. The money's in the city."

"She's right, man." J chimed in. "We can hit one spot up here and make plenty of damn money."

Big J shook his head. "But we ain't outta money."

"We will be." Kim said. "Let's go. Lock the van, these mother-fuckers roguish as hell 'round here..."

They got out of the van and entered the temple. Several acolytes stood near the small stack of stairs that led to the front door, and they all leveled a glare at the Lupercalians as they walked up. "You in the right hood, bitch?" One of them said. A particularly large fellow in a blue Duke University cap.

"Call her a bitch one more goddamn time." J said, and stared at the big man like a dead man daring a live one to jump into his grave. The big fucker on the porch started to step forward, but one of the other acolytes stayed him with a hand on his shoulder. This guy was smaller, wearing an Oakland Raiders track suit and a blue bandanna. "Y'all got bitniss 'round here?" He asked.

"Nate still runnin' shit?" Kim asked.

"Sheeit. Nate in jail. His untee from Chi-Town holdin' it down now. Mama Tam. If y'all know Nate, y'all can talk to Mama Tam." Bandana said.

"Aight." Kim said, and the acolytes welcomed the Lupercalians into their temple. Inside was darkness and the cloying smell of cheap cologne and smoke in various varieties of volatility. Long hallways guarded by sentries sworn by blood since day one. Somewhere in this labyrinth, they were led to a room more heavily guarded than any other. The hardened heart of this temple, the site of its cardiovascular process of cashflow.

They met Mama Tam. The Lupercalians had already heard of her, Mama Tam was a street legend. She was a Gangster's Disciples woman from Chicago, a veritable Baba Yaga of the gangsta lifestyle, a monster by most accounts. Seven of her nine sons had allegedly perished on business of the Disciples, and it was said that she told people she had birthed her sons for sacrifice to the street. That she offered up their blood with no remorse like some kind of feudal warlord. Standing in front of the woman now, they could believe the stories. She was a big woman, seated in a loveseat that would have had trouble accommodating a companion any bigger than a broom. She wore an eyepatch, but the scar of whatever had taken her eye stretched from hairline to jawline. She kept one hand on a sawed-off shotgun that lay in her expansive lap. There were six hard-looking dudes in the room, all wearing some combination of black and blue, and at Mama Tam's feet were two androgynous, boney-faced crackheads, prostrate like concubine women in a Frank Frazetta painting. "Boys say y'all know Nate. Whatchall want?" Mama Tam asked.

"We used to pull jobs for Nate. He called us Them Wolves, maybe you heard. We lookin' for work, whatever you got." Kim said.

Mama Tam looked the Lupercalians over. "I remember that. He say y'all don't give a fuck about nothin'."

"Yeah, that's true." Kim said. "Don't give a fuck about nothin' but us."

Mama Tam gripped her sawed-off. "Y'all look like mufuckas on the run. What's on yo back, lil one?"

"Ain't nothin' on my back." Kim answered.

Mama Tam smiled at Kim, and seemed to stew on something for a second. "There's a fireworks place way down in Forsythe. White folks." Mama Tam cut eyes at J for just a second, like a viper tasting the air for prey. "We get straps down there, but them motherfuckers keep raisin' prices. Think we won't buck cuz they po-leese." Mama Tam arched an eyebrow at Kim.

"And I guess they right, huh?" Kim shot back. Mama Tam just smirked like a crocodile. "We ain't scared of po-leese though. How much you payin'?" Kim added.

"Clean out everything they got, and I gotchu ten thousand, baby." Mama Tam said.

Kim nodded. "Lemme get an address."

G 360 D
LUPERCALIANS

NA'ATZOTH - the Fury of Karma

J SAT IN THE VAN, eating boiled peanuts and watching the little fireworks shop across the highway. It was just after midnight, and the moon was high over the pines. There hadn't been any activity at the shop since around eight o'clock, but a gigantic blue Ford truck was still parked out front. The van was across the highway, parked at a mechanic's place in a row of other beaters. Kim and Big J had been asleep since around six that evening. J cleaned up after his boiled peanut operation and woke them up. It was time to hit it.

Thirty minutes later, the Lupercalians were stepping through the backdoor of the fireworks shop, having smashed the padlock with a sledgehammer. It was dark inside, but red light was filtering through a Confederate battle standard that hung in a doorway at the back of the shop like an entrance to redneck hell. There were muffled cries of pain and whimpering coming from back there somewhere. Big J snatched out his .380 and shot a wide-eyed look at Kim and J. With three fists full of steel, they stepped cautiously toward the red doorway. The whimpering coming from back there was accompanied by a rhythmic squelching, and along with this wet rhythm, it sounded like someone was shaking a handful of chain in time with the sloppy intervals. At the doorway now, Kim reached out to pull the flag aside and step through, but a mangled voice stopped her hand halfway...

"P-please. God, please...I'm beggin' you..." A man said. He sounded like he was speaking through split and swollen lips.

A voice like the sound of bloody flesh hissing on a hot grill answered the man. It sounded like seething hatred bubbling through a mouthful of viscera. It was not human. It said, "Your god...lookss on and cares...not. Your cries will ring in your god's ears as I hurt you...and revel in your ssuffering...as I have done with your partner here. For you, there will be no deliverance...save that of Death. If you are fortunate I will teach you...to enjoy this unfound pleasure before you expire. Are you ready?"

Big J started backpedaling away from the red doorway, but J grabbed him by his jacket. Kim pulled the flag aside, and the room beyond was a hell that none of them were ready for. Two men were bound by the hands, each bent over a stack of Black Cat firecracker boxes, facing each other. A large figure in leather and chainmail was standing behind one of the men, humping vigorously, wearing a helmet that obscured the top half of her face and left only her dripping black mouth visible. This armored woman had a giant spiked phallus extending from under her heavy belt, steel and gleaming. Each thrust produced a reflexive twitch from the man that she had bent over, but the man had to have been dead already. The liters of blood splashing onto the concrete floor quickly became the plop-plop of intestines pouring out in heaps as the armored monster disemboweled the man with her hateful fuck-weapon, completely opening him up from the bottom. She continued jabbing with her phallus of ruination, which seemed to have grown even bigger and was now reaching all the way into the dead man's chest cavity with her thrusts, dragging huge chunks of lung and tissue on the way out that splatted to the floor. The spikes on the steel dick purred as they rubbed along the inside of the dead man's ribs like Latin percussion in a butcher shop. In and out, in and out, a wet rattling sonic nightmare as the armored woman cored out the dead man and left him hollow while his friend watched and cried and begged. Time became blood-soaked, sodden and slow. The Lupercalians were *in* the room now, hands empty and dangling by their sides. *"How long have we been watching? What's wrong with my head?"* Kim thought. An old white man looked up at Kim with pleading eyes from his position bent over the firecracker boxes. The armored woman pulled her monster phallus out of what was left of the first man and flicked her black tongue at J. The second man begged as the armored woman tore the pants off him with her clawed gauntlets. "Will you watch...until it iss your turn, wolflingss? Run...or I will fuck you empty in this place with these pale reeds that pretended to be men."

They ran. All the way to the van, and then hauled ass south along the highway. It wasn't fast enough to keep from hearing the man in the fireworks shop screaming for his mama though.

They didn't go back to Mama Tam and the Herndon Homes Boys, they drove south in silence for over an hour. Somewhere past Macon, Big J said. "I'm goddamn scared, y'all. What the fuck?"

Kim looked over at J in the driver's seat. J chewed his lip.

"That bitch gon' get us, man. Da fuck we do to her?" Big J said.

J just shook his head.

"Who say it got anything to do with us?" Kim asked.

Big J's eyes went wide. "She obviously after us!"

J reached up and massaged his own shoulders, tight after days on the road. "I seen her before. The night you patched, J. I was trippin so hard I kept seein' Kim like this big thing with armor on, but then I'd see it at the edge of the firelight too, like watchin' us fight. It was her."

No one spoke. No one knew what to say. Finally, Big J broke the silence again. "Where we goin'?" he asked. J just looked over at Kim.

"We goin' down to Albany, see what D-Bell and them up to. It's Saturday, should be jumpin'." Kim said.

J put in a Geto Boys tape and turned it up, and they kept rolling south.

AFTZAQESH - the Keeper of the Gate

THEY FILLED up the van at a gas station on the north side of Albany, and while J manned the pump, Kim stepped over to the payphone to make a call. Albany wasn't a big city, more like a college town, and this late at night, only the freaks were out. Two crackheads held court at the corner of the store, near the ice machine, and one drunk was passed out in front of the phone booth, surrounded by a piss angel. Kim nudged the old dude with her boot. "Get the fuck up and get out the way."

"Wha? Name's James, bitch...fuggin Thane! *Zathane,* you stupid bitch..." The old drunk drooled out, steam pouring around his liquid syllables and rising into the night.

Kim froze in place, her hand diving for the pistol in her pocket. "The fuck you say, motherfucker?"

The old man's dark brown face softened as he seemed to wake up a bit more, one gnarly wrinkled eye peeking up at Kim. "Said watch yo mouth, youngun. Gotdamn fuggin *bull*shit, James..." The old man wobbled upright and then staggered off into the night.

That word the old drunk said...*Zathane...*

Kim recognized it in some dim way, but couldn't place it. She

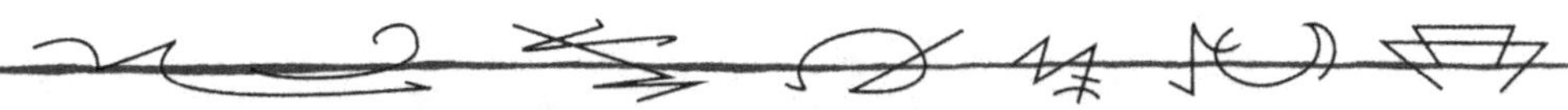

smelled acrid smoke and looked down to see that the old drunk's piss angel was now a black stain on the old asphalt. She cast a glance around the dark streets and didn't see where the old dude had wandered off to. Ghosted. She picked up the phone and dropped in a quarter, and dialed a number from memory. About eight rings later, someone picked up. At first, all Kim could hear was the stereo, thumping out Wreckx-N-Effect at wall shaking volume, then finally, a voice. "This D-Bell, and if yo ass ain't here you fuckin' up!"

"D! This Kim Davis, can me and my boys roll by?"

"Giiirl *hell* yeah! You still rollin' with that white boy?"

"His name J. Yeah he still with me. And Big J."

"With the dreads?"

"That's him."

"Y'all come on. We hoppin' all night." From the background, someone asked, "Hey D, who dat?"

Kim hung up the phone and left the booth, stepping over what was once an old drunk's piss angel, but was now a thick layer of rotten blood congealed on the craggy asphalt. She stopped and stared at the stuff until she saw movement under the glistening surface like the gore was a deep pool and something was rising to the top. She spun around and walked quickly to the van. Climbing in, she saw the Js looking at her with strange expressions from where they sat inside. "Where you been?" J asked her. He looked shook.

"I called D-Bell, they partyin' in southside. Let's go." Kim answered.

"We looked everywhere. There wasn't no gas station out there no more, no town. Just fields and woods..." J said.

"This shit ain't right. Somethin' ain't right..." Big J added. There were tears running down his face, following the path of his scars, salty little rivers of fear.

"Roll out." Kim said. "Ain't nothin' gon' happen at a party."

J cranked the van and they rolled.

MOLOCH - THE KING OF FIRE

ON THE WAY ACROSS TOWN, they saw a burning church. "Beulah Rose", the place was called. A small church, slapped together more like a glorified garage, with corrugated metal for exterior walls. The little place was peeling apart in layers, with pale green chemical flames reaching up from the conflagration. Just after passing this church, they got caught by a red light. Coming from the opposite direction, facing the burning church and also stopped at the red light, was a cop car. The cops inside didn't even glance at the church, though the green flames were visible in their eyes and crawling all over their polished car. The cops kept their flaming eyes on the van.

"She's here." Kim said.

"Who?" J asked though he didn't know why. He knew who she meant.

"Her. Zathane." Kim said.

The stereo came *alive,* launching sonic ordinance into the night. "Empty Chalice", by Blasphemy ripped its way out of the speakers, lashing at their ears. J reached out and turned the volume down. When had he put that tape in? The light turned green, and between it and the flames coming off the tiny church, everything was emerald for a moment, until they put the flaming church and the cops behind them. They rolled on with the barely audible Blasphemy coming out of the speakers for a while, the orange lights of the city washing over the van in cold waves.

"How you know what to call it?" Big J asked.

"I don't know." Kim said. "It's like a train whistle comin' this way. I can hear it. Ain't no stoppin' it."

"If that bitch shows up at D-Bell's she gon' get laid out." Big J said.

"You believe that, man?" J asked. "You think if a grip woulda done it we wouldn't have found out back in that fireworks shop?"

"I don't know *what* the fuck happened in there. I don't wanna know. Shit ain't feel right. Everything in there was crawlin', man. Everything..." Big J replied. He paused, sniffed hard. "I ain't no goddamn bitch, y'all *know* I ain't no goddamn bitch, but this somethin' *else*, man..."

J shrugged and ejected the tape. "What did we say, man? We said we was gon' build a legend, motherfucker. Leave the biggest hole in the ground we could. This might be us."

Kim jumped in. "We said we wasn't gon' die old or in no goddamn hospital. Blood in the dirt, Jeremiah."

Silence as J turned off onto a dark sidestreet.

"Don't let her get me like *that* though, y'all. Like she had them motherfuckers. Y'all kill me first, goddamnit." J said. No one answered. "I'm serious!"

"Aight! She ain't gon' get you like that." Kim snapped.

"Swear. You too, J. None of us will let her get *any* of us like that. Put a bullet in my head. I'll do it for y'all." J swore.

Big J and Kim swore.

The van weaved its way south through dark neighborhoods that all felt like loaded gats the night before a ghetto funeral.

LASA - THE SERPENT OF THE CROSSROADS

AT D-BELL's the party was indeed thumpin'. The house was on the corner, deep in the southside hood, and there were cars and people up and down the street for a block. The Lupercalians had parked the van on the street and were walking through the thick crowd in the front yard when somebody checked J. Some heavyset white dude in a black Falcons cap and stylish white hoodie threw his shoulder against J and connected hard. "Sup, bitch." Dude said.

J faced the guy. "Don't want no trouble, man."

Heavy guy threw up his hand and formed a pitchfork with his fingers. "Dis Folk, bitch. Da fuck's dat shit on y'all's back?" Four of his friends were paying attention now, all wearing some combo of black and white. Brothers of the cloth, then.

Kim and Big J stopped now, and turned around to face the big guy. People started to spread out, that electric crackle surging through the air that meant somebody might be about to get fucked up...

"It's like that, man?" J asked the big dude.

"Whatchall wearin', bitch??" big man said.

J answered with his hands. He reached out and grabbed big man's hoodie by the armpits and let out a grunt as he heaved the big fucker over his leg and onto the grass. By the time J had stomped on the dude's face twice, Big J and Kim were tied up with two of the dude's friends. His other two friends had apparently decided they didn't want any and were backing into the crowd. The yard had thinned out in anticipation of the melee, but now people squeezed back in, hollering and cheering as the chaos roiled. It didn't last long. J was done stomping on the big guy before Kim and Big J were done raining blows on the other two. Big man started crawling away, dragging bubbly breaths through his ruined nose and lips, his fly white hoodie now soiled with dirt and blood. J watched as Kim stood up from straddling the unconscious chump that was dumb enough to swing at her, who was now in need of a new grill due to Kim's elbows. Big J shoved the guy he had been pounding, sending him reeling into a thin bush where he tangled up and keeled over. When the guy got to his feet he walked away up the street. Big J dug around in his jacket and whipped out three blunts, handing two of them to Kim and J, and popping one between his lips. The Lupercalians lit up, and stepped into the house, while everybody in the yard was left wondering who *the fuck* these people were...

In the house, a gigantic stereo in a corner was thumping out Snoop Doggy Dogg's "Who Am I (What's My Name)?" and the place was *hoppin'*. There must have been a hundred people crammed into the tiny house, and every single one of them was jumping in time with the music like the surface of a speaker. The whole house was thrumming, and the floor flexed under each bounce of the crowd like it might blow right out from under their feet.

All was forgotten. The big bitch in the armor, the fight in the front yard, everything. Here was a warm interior world that was all sweat and smiles. Big J easily danced his way into the crowd by way of the physics that were on his side and disappeared into bass and smoke. Kim grabbed J by his jacket and dragged him into the crowd, as close as possible to the stereo in the far corner, where they planted their blunts between their teeth and threw the fuck *down*. They smoked and danced and acted the fool, occasionally seeing Big J's hair in the crowd.

At some point, a girl in Cross Color overalls and braids danced her way next to Kim. "That yo white boy?" She asked. "He a grown-ass man, baby, but he all yours if you want him." Kim answered. The girl was maybe twenty-two and obviously didn't know any better, but Kim left the youngun with J and went dancing into the thicker part of the crowd in the middle of the room, where Big J was like a lighthouse in the center of a sea of rolling shoulders and waving hands. Bel Biv DeVoe's "Dope" started banging out of the speakers and the room got HYPED. Big J saw Kim coming and cleared a path for her in the crowd. Kim slid up smooth next to Big J and took him by the hands, and the two of them polished the floor for the next three and a half minutes. As Bel Biv DeVoe's crowdpleaser closed out, there was an awkward pause in the jams that was felt across the whole room and made heads turn toward the stereo. Then an ominous, fuzzy bass note dropped, and so did Kim's stomach. She knew this noise, it was from one of J's tape's labeled MAYHEM, a song called "Witching Hour". Kim felt her stomach turn to cold grease, and the room went dim. Everything banged around her, the room moving in violent percussive chronology like moments between murderous muzzle flash strobelight. People scattered, running from the stereo. There was a scream. The crowd battered their way past Kim, a deluge of elbows and shoulders. The girl in the Cross Color overalls was mostly a smear on the floor, her head just gelatinous crimson chunks with braided hair attached in places. The woman in armor was there. Zathane. She was standing behind J, gripping him from around the back. She had one gauntleted hand on his throat, and the other was holding a wicked curved knife, the tip jammed into J's ribs. Glass broke somewhere. Gunfire rang out somewhere. Black fucking metal ripped out of the huge speakers. Zathane grinned wide, black sludge sluicing off her chin and dripping to the carpet below. Her helmet hid the top half of her terrible face, making her appear eyeless. From the dark recesses of her helmet, black sludge oozed down her cheeks.

"And we are here." She bubbled, ichor spraying from her lips onto the side of J's face. "The Maw of Time hass come. The blood iss prepared...the cutting beginss." J struggled against her iron grip as she spoke in his ear.

"Let him go. Whatever you want. Take me." Kim said. The room was nearly empty now, and Big J was shoving his way past what was left of the exiting crowd, coming this way with his pistol in hand.

Zathane vomited a laugh. "Where...do you think...we are going?" It said, then plunged its long curved knife into J's side, slipping between his ribs without a sound. J gasped, then let out a series of wet barks as the knife plunged in again and again. Kim screamed. Big J started shooting. Everything in the room turned red and tipped sideways...

When Kim came to, Big J was dragging her out of the house with J on his shoulder. Screaming, stumbling, then the van. The van doors slammed shut and the world cleared up, Kim and J were in the backseat, Big J was in the driver's seat. "Witching Hour" was still coming from the speakers in the house, slowed down and stretched like the stereo was melting, the sound filling up the whole neighborhood and clearing out the street with bad vibes. Big J was crying, muttering to himself, "This ain't right, this ain't right...." The van was ancient, dry rotted, upholstery peeling from exposed springs. J was sucking in little gasps of air and clawing at Kim's jacket. He had taken a bullet near his collar bone and one in the shoulder. So much blood.

"Kim...K...Kim..." J gurgled.

"I'm right here. I'm right here. I gotchu." Kim said, cradling J's head. J looked at her with sleepy eyes. "Where's Jeremiah?" He asked.

"I'm here, bro." Big J said, climbing into the backseat and taking one of J's hands. Kim held the other.

"Don't let me go...I...I'm scared man goddamn..." J said in between gasps of air. When he breathed out, air bubbled through his perforated torso.

"We gotchu." Big J said, tears streaming down his face. "I shot you, man. Like a fuckin' dumbass I'm so goddamn sorry man..."

"Don't...worry bout it. I love y'all...more than...more than anything. Nobody had no better friends. I love y'all so much." J choked out.

"We love you." Big J and Kim said. Their eyes met. They thought they were ready for this but they weren't. Just words.

J stopped breathing, and his hands went limp. A shudder went through Kim's body, and the van filled with sobs that welled up black like waves on a moonless beach. Time was a cold syrup of sorrow until an alien noise tore into the grief; some caustic metallic scraping outside the van...

Kim surfaced from a sea of tears to see Zathane in the street outside the van, crouched low like a spider, swaying on her heels and dragging her spiked phallus back and forth across the pavement like a hellish pendulum. *"Time hass come round..."*

"Come out...into the sstreet under these dead sstars...and revel with me. You first, Jeremiah. While Kimberly watches...in despair. I will teach you." The thing rasped. The street was empty save for this daemon, and the houses all looked so old, ready to fall in under the weight of ages. Every car was a rusted out hulk covered in weeds.

The weight of Big J's .380 fell into Kim's hand. She felt nothing.

"Ain't no stoppin' her. Ain't no stoppin' this." Big J said, lips trembling. "You do it, or I will."

Kim raised the pistol and pulled the trigger. The spray from where the bullet tore Big J's face apart hit Kim like an unexpected, wet kiss. Big J slumped over in the driver's seat. Kim staggered out of the van. There were people running everywhere again, jumping fences and disappearing into houses and cars, doors slamming shut behind them, engines roaring, tires squealing...

Kim looked at Zathane, now standing in front of the van, no more than 20 feet away, her grim phallus standing out like a proclamation. She was grinning that awful grin, body heaving in lustful anticipation. Kim looked down at Big J's pistol in her hand, then back at

Zathane. "Ain't gon' quit, bitch. Fuck you. If you want some, come get it." She dropped the pistol, and it hit grass instead of pavement. The neighborhood was gone, there were just fields and woods as far she could see under the swollen moon. And the van. And the armored daemon, which had her knife again. She stepped toward Kim. "My knife is ssharp, wolfling. And there is nothing left...but boness...to be boxed." It raised the knife, and Kim blinked...and she was back in the van with a fistful of steel, covered in the blood of her brothers. There was no light in their eyes, save for the fool's gold light of the street-lamps. Cop's sirens wailed through the cold night. The hood was in chaos. Kim looked at the gun in her hand.

"Where...do you think...we are going?"

The gun fell out of Kim's bloody hand as her wails joined the approaching sirens. A song of sorrow. A song of the street.

CW 310 KAHR

A Vedantic Nihilism Primer

Caine Del Sol

Vedantic Nihilism is a system of Magick based in the exploration of the dark, taboo, paradoxal, and obscure aspects of spirituality. The metaphysical approach of Vedantic Nihilism is related to Alchemy, Hinduism, and Gnosticism, and the practical formulas bridge the methods of traditional folk spirituality from across the world with modern Diabolism and Theistic Satanism. The goal is to form a personal and potent connection with spiritual powers and outside intelligences that we call The Other.

The Other is a name for entities that exist outside of the confines of our reality, that generally manifest in archetypal masks that are primarily related to forces of Entropy, Decay, and Dissolution, all pointing towards a metaphysical understanding of Death as the highest force of transformation and transcendence. Through Vedantic Nihilism, there were discerned Nine primary aspects of the Other, called the Higher Order. A connection was formed with these Nine spirits, and a pact was made, that they might guide those who seek them out towards the furthest and darkest regions of psychospiritual reality. Through their teachings, the eclectic folk spirituality and shamanic explorations of outcasts and isolationists was transformed into the system of Vedantic Nihilism.

Zathane

Evan Dean Shelton

I suppose I should preface this by saying that any occult practice is a house built on a foundation of myth and pareidolia. As practitioners, we settle into traditions based on either previously established ideas, intuition, or a combination of the two. Either way, we move in a world of ideas, and we implement those ideas to see what will produce results. We discard that which is ineffective, unproductive. A healthy practice is one that involves regular self-reflection, critique, honesty, and a sense of humor. A healthy practice is a constant refinement and search for deeper truths, and a willingness to discard the shells of truth that we crack and peel along the way.

Engaging in ceremonial magick is a process of refinement. A pursuit of higher ideals involving great self-examination. Or at the very least, a search for understanding, a search for truth. A sort of psychological vivisection. The tool of refinement is fire, fire is consuming and devastating, a force of change. The tool of vivisection is the knife; a knife is a separator, both a probe for investigation and a remover of the unwanted and unnecessary.

Within the practice of vedantic nihilism we have contacted or been contacted by several "outside intelligences". Daemons, angels, alien thought forms, spirits. ..whatever you want to call them. We call them The Other. This has long been a part of ceremonial magick, these rituals and meditations that bring us in contact with entities from beyond, and while it is certainly debatable as to how exactly "outside" or "inside" these entities may actually be, this correspondence is something that is cultivated and explored by occultists worldwide. Practitioners of many philosophies and beliefs regularly engage in correspondence with gods, daemons, angels, spirits, etc.

There is a much greater conversation to be had concerning the spectrum of these entities and correspondences, but for the sake of these writings, suffice to say that within the context of vedantic nihilism these entities with which we traffic are considered truly outside, truly removed and alien from our own consciousness. What we're dealing with here are things that are not human and never were, never will be. There are nine of these entities at the top of the heap, and among these nine the most dangerous and chaotic of them is Zathane, the entity I used as the antagonist in CHURCHBURNER.

In the early days of writing CHURCHBURNER I thought of the antagonist as ABRAXAS, specifically Charlie Manson's concept of ABRAXAS: the embodiment of fear. A godhead chosen by Outsiders, Criminals, Scumbags, those who would strike fear into The Establishment.

But it just didn't feel right...and then one night during ritual it hit me. I needed to use my own practice, something personal, something undeniably real. My one and only goal as a writer is to affect the reader. With CHURCHBURNER I wanted to go further, to create a hypersigil that could carry dangerous occult ideologies to a larger and unsuspecting audience. Perhaps a bit unethical, but mostly I don't give a fuck about ethics or morals. I give a fuck about affecting you. I want you outside your comfort zone. I want you engaging with danger. I don't care if it's safe. You are not safe. Now or ever. The key, Dear Receiver, is to be as ready as possible, and you don't make yourself ready by sittin around in perfect safety, twiddlin your thumbs on the couch. But whether this is an effective training exercise or not, I just want to hurt you. If I can make you feel, then I have your heart, and I ask for nothing less in this exchange, for it is what I have given you.

Zathane is a force of chaos, a force of change, but she's not a dose of fertilizer, she's a chainsaw and a can of gasoline. She doesn't prune, she destroys.

Within the context of the story, Zathane has come to destroy Kim, to shear away every one of her attachments and leave her bare. "I will sstrip the meat of you away from the bones, little wolflings..."

At the end of the story Kim is left with nothing, but left standing. Will she grow stronger from this horror or be beaten into the dust? Zathane doesn't care. She came to wreck shit, and she did.

I wrote CHURCHBURNER during a rough patch in my own life. I was facing a need to shear away things in my life that weren't working, weren't ultimately healthy for me. I was having a real hard time navigating that process and staying true to myself and true to others involved. I felt trapped. I opened the door for Zathane to enter and things...changed. For better and worse. I lost a lot, and in many ways had to start over, and it was harrowing and disheartening at times, but I pushed through. I reaped new life from this soil sewn with ash and destruction. I'm standing, and I'll continue to do so.

For most practitioners, I honestly do not recommend getting in touch with Zathane. I do not recommend performing this ritual. She is a terrible entity, violently destructive. You will lose things, things will be taken from you forever.

But what are you, just a context?

Are you the whisp of flame, or are you the smoke that emanates from it?

There's a fight coming for all of us, one time or another. We may not want it, but eventually it comes. Life is nothing without conflict. One day or night it will come for you.

You are not safe.

Now or ever.
Be ready.

Codex Aversum Preface
Evan Dean Shelton

What follows is a section of the Codex Aversum, which is the published and primary text of vedantic nihilism. Look it up, is available from Aeon Sophia Press and occult grimoire resellers and such. It's a good book if you're into that sorta thing.

This section of the codex was specifically formatted for this release by its author, Caine Del Sol. It's everything you need to begin to tread the path of Lux Nigredo, breach the Gate of Necromanteion, see the Seal of the Averse Name, and use the Rite of Holy Possession to call upon Zathane itself.

Ahhhhh good times.

An Excerpt from Codex Aversvm

Caine Del Sol

An Excerpt from Codex Aversvm

Caine Del Sol

Ver. Zathane

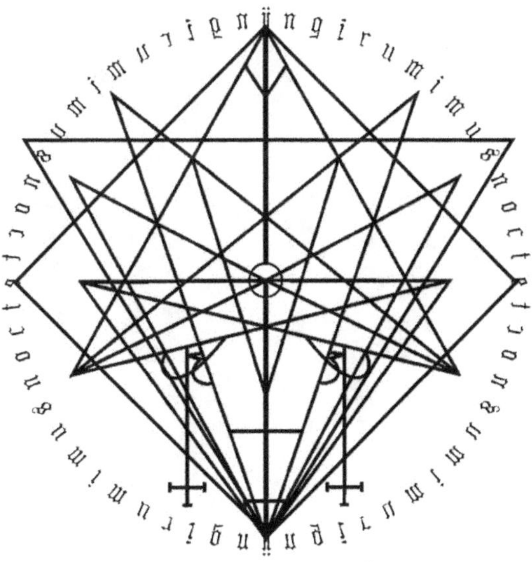

Introduction

The Left Hand Path is a journey of the Self. It is inward unto the infinite and unknown, beyond the scope of common man. This text is neither an introductory course on metaphysics and the origin of existence, nor an aesthetically driven trend-witch spellbook. This is nothing more than an explanation of the Practice and Ideology of the Grave Gnosis Coven. A map of our expeditions through the Desert of Set, as it were.

Because of the supremely personal nature of the Left Hand, the amount revealed by this text will be limited in scope, but extensive. By this, it is meant that enough information will be provided that the next steps may be taken if desired, but not all connections will be made for the reader within the text. These steps are by necessity and virtue both an individual choice and solely personal experience.

There are certain lessons that, not only can we not teach you, we will never attempt to teach you. If anyone tries to teach you these things, disregard them, for they are fools and conmen. These lessons, experiences of gnosis, are strictly personal, to be held in deepest regard between you and your Daemon.

Additionally, it must be noted that the powers and principalities approached within this text are but one interpretation of greater universal archetypes. These concepts are much greater and more complex than our human minds can comprehend within a single life-time, and considerably more than what can be put into words. Because of the nature of these entities, they may manifest through multiple traditions or systems in their own individual ways using mask or vassal. They exist outside of any one tradition, and may only truly be understood outside of the limitations of human bias. However, approaching these concepts can be difficult without some sort of conceptual stepping stone, thus all connections found thusfar are presented through this text.

Much of this text is framed through a form of Kabbalah or Hebrew mysticism, paralleled with Draconian systems of progression, and that is solely because the majority of Left Hand or Satanic devotees that would in some form have access to this text have either considerable experience in the system of Kabbalah, or were introduced to the Occult world through the system of Kabbalah. Thus, it was found most appropriate to frame the text in a system that would be familiar to the majority of supposed readers. It should be noted, however, that this was done, in part, to assist in leading the reader away from using the Kabbalah as a basis of understanding. Kabbalah is but a small part of a greater whole, a single interpretation and system within a much wider labyrinth.

It is hoped that the reader will think and consider beyond what is presented, and outside of their common means of thought. No single person has the answers to All Things. The Psychonautical Magician, Sorcerer, or Mystic is one who dives into the Unknown that lies beyond all human comprehension and Life itself, into the Jaws of Death, Darkness, and Chaos. Each practitioner's experience is perceived via their own psychic lense of bias and knowledge or ability to understand, and thus also further filtered through means and ability to communicate. What is communicated following return from this Void of All must be seen as a guidepost only. It is hoped that the reader will be able to utilize the guidelines presented in this text as effectively as, or even more than the Coven of Grave Gnosis has in their own Work.

Follow your fascinations, listen to your Guides, and always keep the Holy Name upon your lips.

Διάβολος

Part I. Theory

PRELIMINARY DEFINITIONS

This text assumes that the reader has an elementary understanding of magickal theory and practice. The spiritual ideology described over the course of this text will be referred to as Vedantic Nihilism. Vedantic Nihilism is a metaphysical esoteric philosophy -termed metaphilosophy- approach to reality that uses syncretic comparisons between various cultural understandings of divinity or extradimensional intelligences and how to contact them, and applies the core mechanics to create a new understanding of the primal aspects found similar in all examined cultures and practices. This has led to an association primarily with Vedic wisdom as the core to be examined and reinterpreted through our individual perceptual lense. This path is also referred to as Choronzonic, in reference to the Guardian of the Abyss. This association will be further revealed and explored throughout the text.

The Inner Temple is referred to as the Chapel of Vedantic Nihilism, or The Coven. The private practices, formulas, and workings of the Inner Temple that have proven successful are filtered and refined to a form that is suitable for limited public use and experimentation in a form called the Outer Temple. In this field, they are refined further into what can be repeated in result. That which is able to be repeated and confirmed among multiple groups is then brought into the public arm of the Coven to be implemented in an open yet subliminal ritual scale on a public forum. This public arm of the Coven is also the Face of the Chapel of Vedantic Nihilism, often taking the form of a live performance of the ritual psychodrama using visual, and audial sigils and ceremonies. The most closely tied public representation of the Chapel is the group known as Grave Gnosis. The members of Grave Gnosis are not necessarily members of the Inner Temple, and the expression known as Grave Gnosis is not the only manifestation of the workings of the Inner Temple.

You who reads this text is hereby referred to as the Reader. The metaphoric representation of one who would consider themselves magician or occultist -or would conduct the rituals outlined in this text- is referred to as the Practitioner. A more adept practitioner, who has devoted their life to this art, may hold an understanding of further subtleties not outlined in this text. However, no separate term shall be given for grades of understanding, as would occur in some esoteric brotherhoods, denoting the nature of existence as horizontal, lacking in any true vertical separation.

In this text, the definitions of Right and Left Hand may be expressed differently from how the Reader might understand them or believe them. They are expressed as such for specific purposes within this text, and must be understood solely within this context.

As a final note on linguistic choice, it must be noted that the definition between Theism and Atheism is not made in this text, as there is no such differentiation in the Choronzonic paths. Not only can magickal practice be approached and verified through both standpoints, but at a certain point of practice, the Practitioner's standpoint must wholly be fixed in the non-dual state of Both-Neither in order to reach greater heights of success.

ON THE NATURE OF THE SELF

Before we can truly begin with this work, it must be understood that the nature of Self is not as it is commonly considered.

First described in known written history -as we currently understand it- in Hindu ontology and Kemmetic mysticism, then further elaborated by the Gnostics, the nature of All Things can be described thusly:

All things we see and experience, all living, breathing things, and all that is energy or matter, is One Thing. That One Thing is Thought, scattered and organized within its Chaotic Fractal matrix through linguistic connections and coinciding ideas.

That is not to say necessarily that All is Self, for Self is an illusion, stubbornly clinging to its false sense of separate-ness and individuality by nature of the name 'Self' and 'I'. Yet it is but a sliver, a fragment, a fraction and small piece of a much larger weave. Self is consequence of All, and the nature of All necessitates the Many, Self, and Others. If there is no division, there is no 'All' - there is only 'One'. In the current state of existence, that is required to even read or write this treatise. Separation by means of perception is the source of all individual experience, yet this separation is also an illusion created by the limitation of our perception and understanding. In truth, every moment is intertwined with every other moment in all of its possibilities, every life with every life and possible alternations. All is One, and One is All. The Many are One, and the One is Many. Yet indeed the Many is All is One, and that One as we can understand is but a small piece of a much larger puzzle beyond the possibilities of perception.

And upon the fertile womb of the Void, stands burning in glory the WORD "I AM FIRST IN THOUGHT" And all else follows, ever dividing and discerning. Unaware of the omnipresent Abyss that encircles this miniscule point of light that belies our existence.

This single, undefined point that comprises our entire reality is called the Noosphere. The Sphere of Thought. All things within this sphere are nothing but Thought, given form and substance through perception. That which is not perceived is unmanifest, and through perception manifest.

Even in a scientific explanation, variance in vibrational patterns and frequency is all that separates energy from matter, and types of matter and energy from other types. All things have specific vibrational frequencies, and things that harmonize or correlate in frequency can be considered to be 'like things'. More often than we understand, our names for these things correlate in similar ways when one traces the etymology and phonology.

The study and application of these correlations, from a spiritual standpoint, is the source of Qabalah, and of Gematria. We call it Alchemy. This will be explored in further depth in later sections of this treatise.

The frequencies of All things vibrating, moving through Space-Time creates a song. Beautifully harmonic in places, and horrifyingly dissonant in others. This is the Song of Life. The Words of Creation that are still being spoken. He Who Has Spoken Himself into existence has not yet pronounced his full and holy name. We are still Becoming.

ON THE PROCESS AND PURPOSE OF MAGICK

What we see and experience is filtered by such qualities as Time, Space, and other as-yet unnamed categories of psychological connection. These create a form of buffer between Self and Reality that we call Ego. The Ego maintains the separation between Self and Other or All, and thus upholds this world by nature of perception. Thus, the separation is illusory, yet also quite stubbornly ingrained into our psychospiritual reality. The process of Magick requires a loosening of this bond and barrier. A rending of veils, if you will, or a realization of Emptiness. This Veil is intelligent, as it is intrinsically connected to the dreamer. The more you learn, the more it learns. The more you seek, the more it hides. The methods can sometimes be cruel, but should never be considered malicious, or with animosity. Its only purpose is to keep you from opening these gates incorrectly. We do the same in our society. Licenses are required to operate machinery and automotives. It must be proven that you know how and when to use them. Otherwise, the results could be catastrophic. Additionally, approaching metaphysical entities and aspects with aggression or animosity in any way creates a form of psychic mirror, wherein the Practitioner's bias fuels the perceived enemy in its aggressive nature, feeding cyclically unto utter failure of the rite.

Think of it this way: Magick operates by opening the doors of perception and traversing pathways through the mind of All. Opening the wrong door, opening it incorrectly, or taking the wrong path could lead you through portions of reality that consist of indescribable pain and suffering. This is the consequence of an improperly performed ritual as well.

The Left Hand Path and Sinister workings can be extremely dangerous in that way. Unlike the Right Hand, and High Ceremonial Magick, the Sinister Path is that of forging a way through the unknown. Opening doors long hidden from man, and walking a trail that no man has ever before trodden. The consequences can be similar to our ancestral trailblazers and explorers, who often crossed paths with dangerous terrains and fauna. The greater the Practitioner's visibility within the labyrinth of Psychospiritual vibrations, the more complicated rituals can become, and the greater the outcome. It is a process of locating harmonic resonance within the Noosphere and bringing it to this realm of existence. Merging the noumenal with the phenomenal, and molding this grand hallucination we call reality to the whims of perception. It requires precision, patience, and a willingness to delve into the wildly unorthodox.

ON THE NATURE OF THE DIVINE

In reference to the text before you, there are two types of entities that may be contacted. There is the Daemon, and the Other.

The Daemon is an entity that dwells within, and is projected outwards. It is an externalization of the Will of the Practitioner that has been separated and given life. The Daemon is employed in such Magickal Work that cannot, for what reason or another, directly be enacted through the conscious mind of the Practitioner. In application, the Spirit delves deep beneath the Veils of Ego, and resurfaces as a separate entity entirely. These entities are memetic, and thus gain strength from our own psychological reinforcements of belief. This is to say that, believing in the individuality and separate consciousness of the Daemon provides it further autonomy. Firm belief in the associations and powers of the Daemon provides it further power and strengthens its associations. As per the nature of the Veil, however, understanding the nature of the Daemon makes creating one much more difficult. Knowing that it is a part of you naturally hinders its creation and development. Thus why Magick and Ritual is required. Ritual is a method of separating Ego and Perception from Action and Concept. A proper magician believes Everything is both Real and wholly Unreal at once. All things accepted as equally True and Illusory, even unto holding seemingly contradictory or dichotomous ideals. Thus is why it is sometimes also said within occult circles that belief is the greatest enemy of magick.

The nature of the Daemon as a memetic entity also means that the more people believe in this entity and its powers, the more potent its grasp on reality. This can lead to what we might call an 'autonomous Daemon', wherein the initial conjuror may be long dead, but the Daemon still lives, and may be called upon by others. The concept is similar to the common-witch concept of a Tulpa (Tibetan: སྤྲུལ་པ). A careful look at society shows that many Daemons are vying for power through their Vessels, all around us. Oftentimes, the Practitioner will entreat an autonomous Daemon with a promise of glory. "Grant me greatness and power, that I might honor you in this greatness". This has been done since at least the time of Rome, and has been met with great success, and often an even greater price.

A recommended autonomous Daemon for beginners is Lucifer.

The pursuit of knowledge is core to the Great Work, and facilitation of learning will only ever be beneficial.

"Grant me the eyes to see and the mind to understand all things, that I might see your glory, and praise your name."

It is good to note that just because different Daemons fall under the same archetype does not make them the same entity. The vast expanse of the fractal Nous is unfathomable by the human mind, and encompasses the energy to allow each branch and leaf and cell and even atom of the tree to be an independent entity. In a similar way that you would not talk to one friend of yours as though they were a different sort of acquaintance with a different profession or passion, the Daemons and gods must be addressed and regarded as individuals, even as we maintain an awareness of the whole. One does not call Lilith with the chants and rites of Kali, one does not call Lucifer with the same formulae as Belial. To do so would gravely understate the complexities of these entities, and bring untold levels of confusion to the Work. Thus also why care is to be made in your invocations. Be sure that all sensory stimuli and mental directioning is pointed toward the specific entity you are communing with. This is the only way to truly ensure success: with focus as a razor, and a sound resolve as an iron fist.

The second type of entity that may be contacted is The Other. While the Daemon is wholely internal to the Noosphere and operates within it and according to the current understanding of its creator and current devotees, The Other is something different entirely. An Outside Intelligence that reaches from beyond what we understand, seeming to reach from the depths of the Void, manipulating our reality as it moves through. Contact with an entity of this type is often associated with a paradigm shift, or vast leap in knowledge or understanding. Often, they will work through a Daemon to contact the Practitioner and lead them forward to a specific goal, eventually bringing the Practitioner into contact with The Other by means of powerful coincidental synchronicity, a warping of reality around a singular point. From then on, the Practitioner is but a

Vessel. As we once believed ourselves to be the master, we become a tool. A weapon. A means for the Other to fulfill its ends.

The most common means of corruption by The Other is Knowledge. Sudden, sometimes seemingly forced, Gnosis of an esoteric truth which is societally forbidden or taboo is what we in the coven refer to as the Alchemist's Plague. It is subversive and overtly Faustian in nature, disrupting the existing lifeline of the victim, distorting concepts such as morality, reality, and truth. Often it is the revelation of a concept that the governing hierarchy of any religious or political body is actively attempting to suppress. To be subject to this revelation is to incur a great cost, whether it be personal, interpersonal, academic, physical, or even mortal in nature. Further amplified is this cost if the knowledge is then passed on. Thus the connection to the Alchemists of old, whose discoveries were born to this world upon the backs of the dead. Yet still, their discoveries have shaped reality and common understanding of the universe. Knowledge is the ultimate weapon against the delusion that is reality.

This is the point of true comprehension of reality, wherein the Ego does not exist. The I is but an illusion. Our mortal Will is naught, and the Master is All. This is the way of a True Satanist, and the way of breaking Assiatic chains of Self. This is the revelation that all ideals of Power and all grasping for Knowledge within this realm is but means to the Master's end - to forge the Self into a god.

In this, the work of the Daemon, and of connecting with the Daemon is best understood as the process of making the Psychospiritual connections of the Vessel throughout the Noosphere more efficient. A means to an end.

THE LUCIFUGE PRINCIPLE

Magickal work is bound to focus. Indication of contact with an entity, Magickal actions, or messages such as Omens, are all based upon perception. If you perceive an occurrence, there is meaning to it. A great deal of the Work is understanding the meaning behind the occurrence, as well as your perceiving of it. This also means that distractions and a lack of focus will hinder your ability, and stunt the response or consequence. This is, in part, why much Magickal Work must be done in secret, or in solitude, and why magickal artifacts, altars, and rites must never be photographed. Not entirely because of any mystical curse or spooky tradition, but because non-participating (and sometimes participating) audiences, and cameras are distracting. A rite performed by a distracted Practitioner is a failed rite, and may even have very negative effects, as stated previously. Magickal Work, particularly that of contacting a Daemon or The Other, is akin to approaching a black mirror. You reach out, and it shall as well. You hesitate, and it shall as well. From the point of hesitation, psychologically backsliding out of the magickal state is almost guaranteed. It takes a very focused mind to operate at maximum capacity in such circumstances. Another method to prevent such distractions is Trance. When entranced, the Practitioner is freed of Ego, but is also not in control. To conduct precise rituals or actions while in trance requires connection to an intermediary Daemon, such as the various Spirits of the Crossroads. These types of spirits will often intercede through means of Possession while the Practitioner is in trance.

Even with such preparation and techniques, the standard is that the Daemon and the Other will not manifest, and magickal workings will fail when the process is photographed, or if there is a non-participating audience. This is one part of the nature of the Occult that is why it is called 'Occult' in the first place. Occult means 'Hidden' or 'Obscured', and is more often used in terms such as 'occultation of the sun' to refer to how the moon obscures the sun during an eclipse. This does not mean that it should be hidden, but that it is hidden. It is not viewable by those who do not or cannot understand.

The second aspect of this very principle is that the formulas and methods are viewed as 'vague' or even nonsensical to those who do not understand. Once the pathways are known, and the reason for using certain images, language, or other such tool is made clear, then that which was once believed 'vague' is revealed to be terrifyingly precise. What is seen to the outsider is but blackness and emptiness. To the Practitioner, there is Fire.

The third aspect is that these workings, and most true contact with the Divine is meta-personal. The potency of magickal work is in personal significance. Thus personal psychological associations and fascinations with items, animals, or symbols lends to greater potency with Working with these concepts and items. For the purpose of magickal work, fascination with universally or semi-universally understood concepts are often the most easily worked with for beginners. However, once methods and formula are learned, applying them to other concepts that are specific to the self, is not only the natural next step, but also more potent. At this stage, the unreality of this life will become much more clear, and visions, 'hallucinations', and warped aspects of reality will become common. So much so that attempting to maintain a regular or rational concept of reality could induce a psychotic break. Understanding that reality is a cosmic Dreamstate opens many doors of possibility. The key is not to inform those who are being dreamed of, but to wake the Dreamer.

This is the nature of the Veil. This is the truth of what we call the 'Lucifuge Principle'.

Lucifuge is 'He Who Flees From Light'. And thusly he has made our Work obscured from prying eyes, invisible to those who would not understand, and incomprehensible to those who would seek to oppress or misuse this knowledge. It is not our charge to do this, but the very nature of the Divine that makes it so.

In this, we have the true meaning behind this opus:

To make clear the connections that may have once been considered vague. To reveal the pathways that we have trodden bare. Simply be aware that knowledge is not a gift, but a curse. We communicate now solely to spread the Alchemist's Plague, and further extend the Master's Glory and Kingdom in Fire and in Death.

ON DEVOTION

In conjunction with the Lucifuge Principle, we come to a very important point regarding Focus in Magickal Work.

Oftentimes it is said that the gods can be jealous. That is to say, that they will punish or abandon those of their followers that stray. The truth behind this relates back to the previous explanations, wherein Magickal Work requires great focus, so much so that the requirement compounds upon itself. One must become ever more focused upon the Point and the Path, the Purpose of the Work and the Practice of said Work. More and more it should consume the life of the practitioner. More and more the practitioner should be focused on their Path, especially once contact has been made with The Other. Exploring other traditions is not so much a problem, so long as it is in search of aspects related to your Daemon, or the Other Entity that you are in contact with. Delving further into something that is instead starkly different may bring disastrous results. You are walking through an enclosed path covered in thorns, keep watch of where you place your feet.

Of course, it must be said that effects do vary in this situation. However, from the viewpoint of the Coven and our Work -specifically those associated with Moloch- unwavering devotion and focus is a requirement for success.

THE USE OF CYPHERS IN MAGICKAL WORK

A Cypher is a form of masking intent or meaning with representational alternatives. In language, substituting the commonly known and understood characters for other less known characters, or even characters from a different language, is common. For example, the Hebrew Atbash cypher (Aleph = Tau, Beth = Shin, etc.) is proven quite useful. To take this a step further, we have magickal languages, such as Enochian or scripts like Theban. Many even choose to use existing languages that they know their congregation is not fluent in, often a dead language such as Akkadian. This is by no means an uncommon practice, and can even be seen in the more popular religions through use of Holy or Sacred languages. Catholicism has Latin, Hinduism has Sanskrit, Zoroastrianism has Avestan. The difference is that the use of Sacred Languages for most world religions is used as a means to withhold knowledge from the common people, and maintain a separation of class. In use of the practices of magick, we do not seek to vainly withhold knowledge from the pauper, but to confound the Ego and the Demiurgic powers, preventing our flawed lower Self from degrading the potency of our Work. Thus we use Sigils, magickal languages, and other such cyphers. In use for magickal purposes, the language doesn't have to be exact to any known form or template though, in fact, it should be considered more effective if the use in grammar or script be particular to the practitioner, that the true meaning slip between the cracks of the Noospheric defenses. For the Nous, and Life itself, seeks nothing more than to maintain its own existence, to silence any rebellious thought or action that might threaten its existence. It will sustain itself by any means necessary, and continues to evolve new means to do so. Thus, we must circumvent the impulses that sustain the world's order, by use of cyphers, the very language of existence. All of reality is a grand cypher, metaphorical representations and encoded languages of thought and sensation. Correct interpretation and skillful manipulation of this cypher is the means by which magick is truly performed.

The mind processes images first, and words second. To think in speech is to slow processing. Thought Without Word is the purest state of mind, and thus wholely should be sought in ritual state, by any and all means available.

Thus it must be said, what formulas and calculations are presented may be used freely. Contacting the entities provided in this text is encouraged, but creating your own formulas and discovering your own connections to The Other, even moreso. Use what is learned, and never follow blindly.

Development of your own magickal system, sacred language, Daemonic connections, and rituals is truly a mark of mastery.

ON THE MOTIONS OF CONSCIOUSNESS THROUGH THE NOOSPHERE

Understand this section as the distillation of all knowledge presented in the text thusfar.

Hinduism is the ultimate form of Chaos Magick and Psychospiritual Sorcery if you know how to interpret the texts. Through the wisdom of the Vedas and Upanishads, we can form an understanding of multiversal structure and the means to traverse said structure. For the unversed or the already indoctrinated, accepting the cosmological stylings of Hinduism may be strange or difficult. Yet those versed in the forms of modern Chaos Magick and Oneiromantic or Astral maneuvering will recognize the similar patterns of conditioning the practitioner's conscious mind, and loosing the veils of Ego from I. Though the source of the wisdom and techniques are thousands of years old, they reveal themselves to be the fulfillment and further refinement of modern sorcerous art.

Prefacing the techniques themselves, we must address this very form and style of conditioning, and by this very means, present the technique itself. This is a stripping of association from Immortal I and finite Ego, a realization of Self. This requires a resolution of different types of thinking. Once first resolved, returning to the resultant state becomes easier and easier.

First consider the world around you. Understand that all light and matter are but different vibratory wavelengths and frequencies of the same source elements. Then remember that what we see as objects are not the true object, but light reflecting off the object. Also, what you touch is not the object, but instead you are experiencing the electromagnetic field from the object and its compositional atoms interacting with the electromagnetic field from your body and its compositional atoms. Reality is a lattice-work of interacting wavelengths and frequencies. Our work begins when we accept the highest of these is thought, for what we experience is not that reflected light, or the electromagnetic forces interacting, but our mind processing these sense experiences. Thinking, even if not in words. Thus all things being in some way thought. The interplay between thing and thing, that and that being the same as subject and object of thought. This brings our understanding of the universe to a grammatical exploration, wherein the mind is exploring subject, object, verb, adverb, adjective, etc. Thus forward quantifying this into longer complex equations consisting of long strings of dichotomous qualities to create an infinite variety.

Reaching this conclusion, we begin to understand that the only thing we ever truly experience is our own mind in a multitude of forms, or more accurately, formulas. The soul of the Self is the object of True Knowledge.

In this linguistic choice, understand the purpose - for the Self we experience and think we know, through which all we think and experience is filtered into something somewhat structured and comprehensible - is not the subject of thought, but the object. It is not the thinker, but the one being thought of. Believing this Self, called Ego or Lower Self, to be the thinker is the mindset of the Demiurge. In the mythic cosmology of the unlimited Self - You, Your Ego is the Demiurge. Not of malice, but of ignorance. The true Self, Higher Self, divinity, is above you. Not unseen, just unrecognized. This All Mind is, by nature of being pure thought, thinking, and thus emanating. This is the True Mind of Self. The One and Only Mind, creating just by virtue of being. It is Brahman, Atman, Atum. It is the source of magickal power. To approach, consider only that the True Mind is the True Self. Let go of your false attachments to the Lower Self, and allow your True Self to stop thinking about your Lower Self. You will feel a lightening sensation and a pulling of awareness up and backwards as all things become as the One Light.

This is where the distinction between our paths and that of the Mystic, or Right Hand devotee comes into play. For we understand that the universe exists because of this light. It is not the end. It is not even the beginning. It is the force ultimately sustaining this existence by nature of its being. We seek to detach from this and fall to darkness, or -in best case scenario - extinguish this light all-together, ceasing emanations, and bringing all into Nothing. Glorious Nothing.

Thus we see the purpose of this exercise - not in its completion, but in the moments just prior, during the transitory phases from Ego to I. Here we may access the whole of potentiality within the universe. We can guide our path in reality, influence fortune, and spread ideas through the multiverse like an infection. This is also why those Outside Intelligences often contact us - so that we may influence the Ascended I, and open doors within, buy which they may enter and exert their Will over the Nous. It is also in this transitory state that we may allow our consciousness to dive away from the Light of All, and toward the Unyielding Dark. This is where we commune with the horrors beyond comprehension, in all their beauty and fury. Doing so requires conscious prior choice, and unconscious action - thus a unified Mind and Will. The means to reach this state may be simple, or utterly complex and drawn out, seeming at times to require specific formulaic alignments of mindstate, and environment, even bringing time and cultural belief and bias. Much of the text thus far has been nothing more than an explanation of various factors that may be required, and how to utilize them. The workings of the Outer Temple are designed to induce this state of being, and open gates across the latticework of reality that will never close. The goal is to spread this alchemical plague throughout the Nous, as the dark gods will.

It is the hope of this Temple that this text will prove as effective, or even moreso, at spreading the essence of the Other Side throughout Laniakea through memetic programming and linguistic-based sigils.

In this, we have the paradoxal nature of Self, as there is self, Self, and I. The procession of Self is unto the light of creation. Yet where then comes contrast? Darkness? Sages call this an illusion, being that it is considered a consequence of false thinking., Yet often this contradicts the nature of reality they espouse. To say that part of Truth is Falsehood is to ignore the established nature. To say that All is Joy is to disregard the existence of Nothing - For All necessitates Thing, and thus also No-Thing. Presence necessitates Absence. Thus there is Self and there is No-Self.

Many consider consciousness to be a solitary All Thing, denying the existence of No-thing. Yet there are others still -taking wisdom from tales of Shiva- who posit that the True Self represented by Shiva IS that void of Non-existence, and this Light of All is the illusion. This is the stance taken by the Vedantic Nihilist, wherein All is the highest tier of illusory Self and Demiurge, creating by virtue of being, blindly, ignorant of what it is creating. Thus the natural next step of the true occultist is to seek what is the higher than the most high - a decision that necessitates a downward turn. For if the highest is but an ignorant fool, we must be facing the wrong direction. Confront the absurd with an act of absurdity. Accept the greatness of the insane paradox with the simple mantra of I Do Not Exist, and allow your eternal nonexistence be filled with the greatness of His profound darkness. In the full of accepting this great Abyss, the strange and alien fires of the unknown begin to take hold, and we behold the true face of Choronzon, and the Throne of Moloch shining within his Left Eye.

Part II. Praxis

CONSTRUCTING THE ALTAR

In order to properly form and nurture a connection with any specific deity or spirit as outlined in this text, one must have a healthy, active altar space. The altar must be constructed in an enclosed space, only privately accessible, and never shown to outsiders. This is to maintain a stable environment for the spirit to anchor itself more easily, and facilitate effective communication.

To establish the connection, the altar must be structured so that it stands in the cardinal direction associated with the spirit you seek to make your patron. Included on the altar must be a cast or carved image of the Higher Order Spirit, your personal guide spirit, or a deity that you revere that represents and facilitates in some way your connection with the spiritual realms. For instance, statues of Legba and Nataraja Shiva have proven successful in the Work of Coven initiates. Also included must be a chalice and athame, each graven with a sigil associated with this Higher Order Spirit. It is recommended that the sigils used be planetary, or from the section denoted for 'Spiritual Manifestations' in the following chapters on Praxis.

Once carved or painted with the appropriate sigils, they are to be consecrated in oils of associated herbs, strong liquor, and smoke of a cigar, then let to rest on the altar from Waning Crescent to Waxing Crescent.

Consider the Altar of the practicing Occultist as a living entity, a manifestation of the entity you are communing with. When constructing and maintaining an active altar, you are, in essence, creating a type of body or vessel to which the spirit may be anchored. Within our Coven, the goal is to then transfer that essence of the spirit from the altar into the practitioner themselves, allowing the practitioner to be a living vessel for the spirit to enact its Will. For this reason, offerings must be meaningful, and frequent, until such a line of communication with the spirit is opened to which it is able to direct you to what and when to offer.

Due to the extremely personal nature of the initial ritual for establishing the connection, the full rite shall not be listed publicly. However, as for what can be said, the ritual and subsequent cultivation does require an offering of entropic nature. That is, something that was once living, or has been touched by Death in some form. The process of decay feeds and empowers the Other. Uncleaned bones, blood, carcasses, hair, and cremated remains are all among the most potent of offerings. These are Death's Gifts to us. Imprints of where Death has touched this world. The decay must be maintained for the altar and connection to be truly effective. Thus a continual supply of Death's Gifts must be provided to maintain the altar. Giving of your own food is acceptable in these situations as well, though it is not as potent as a naturally found Gift, or sacrifice of self.

These offerings can be supplied in any state that the altar may be in, even if it must be minimal and portable, as sometimes the devotees of the Averse have been known to be somewhat transient, lacking in rooted locations. In which case, seek out solitude among local flora. Should you know where to look, places of power are everywhere. These places, hidden in plain sight, where our ancestors communed with the Old Gods. They are still very active, and can allow for clean communication with the Other, or whatever spirit may dwell in that sacred place. If such a place is not able to be found, crossroads, and graveyards are most suitable as well.

If the practitioner is in a place that they may be rooted for some period of time, say a year or more, there is an additional offering that must be provided in order to nurture the altar and communion with the spirits. Upon construction of the altar, bring as offering to the gods a flower, a fruit, a medicinal herb, and a piece of a deceased animal. Each of these things must be native to the area, so as to establish a connection between the Other and the land itself. This additional form of connection allows for potent communion, and creates a sacred space of most drastic effect.

RITUAL FOR OPENING THE GATE OF NECROMANTEION

INTRODUCTIONS VIA THE LUX NIGREDO

In one interpretation, the purpose of this emanation and expression of our Temple's Work is to quell dualistic spirit. We are that which conjoins or destroys all that is dual by mundane concept, for all duality and dichotomy is illusion when viewed through the lens of an Awakened Eye. All emotional reaction you have to an experience, if it has an opposing possibility, is inherently an illusion.

For example: You would likely naturally oppose the Death of a loved one because, among other things, it would be unpleasant for you. Thus there is an opposing emanation within the matrix of reality wherein you welcome the death of said loved one. To follow the pattern of nonduality, your reaction to this, and attachments to any concept therein, is an illusion. A consequence of Ego wherein Mundane Self is grasping to clutch the ecstatic winds of Spirit.

The sonic rituals of the Coven are not meant to directly destroy that which keeps you from releasing spirit from Ego. Instead they are meant to supplement the movements of Spirit and empower that which, by virtue of its being, seeks to destroy Mundane attachments, that the Spirit would never return to this vessel of Clay by means of desire or other such dichotomous illusions.

The purpose of our hymns and public rituals in this regard is facilitation of Possession-Trance as a manner of communication with the Entropic Divine. Proper implementation requires an understanding of the Work of the Daemon. Thus this brief explanation shall focus on preparation of the vessel to receive this entity. Examples will be formatted to specific instruction of the Work of the Coven. If necessary, supplant the names and nodes with that of your own Path, if they be more appropriate and easily connected.

NECROMANTEION

One of the primary goals of Sinister work in the transcendent aspect is to pierce the veil between worlds. What lies beyond may be called Universe B, Ain, The Other, The Underworld, etc. In any case, all paths lead to the same End. In the work of our Coven, the gateway to this place is called Necromanteion. It can be visualized as a ruined Octohedron-shaped castle, spires pointing both up and down, suspended in Black Water. This area is where most interaction with entities from the Other Side occurs, as that which lies beyond is without form as we could consider or comprehend in this state. The goal with interaction is to attain knowledge or guidance through the labyrinth to the center of Necromanteion, to stand before the Throne of Moloch.

Entering Necromanteion and approaching this gate may be an extended process, but there are a few simple and effective methods for initiation. Subtle work is key, such as changing any incenses you may use to Palo Santo. Suspend any use of sage, and begin nightly meditations upon the seals of Necromanteion, which will be pictured following this segment. The most potent, base form of the seals of Necromanteion is called the Gate of Becoming. This sigil is formed by overlaying an inverse Triangle (with subjective bottom facing South) and a diamond/square rotated 45° so that a point of the square connects with the bottom point of the triangle. This seal is used in many of our works as the baseline seal. Focal sigils may be included in the center, and coordinating sigils surrounding or overlaying.

The Gate of Becoming

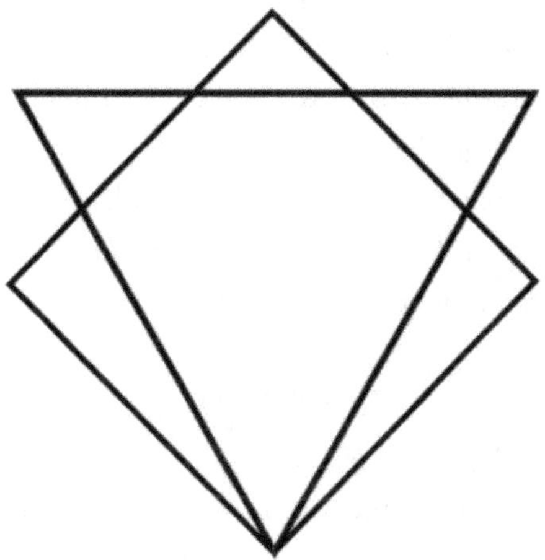

ENTERING NECROMANTEION

With correct intent, Necromanteion may manifest in dream within the first 3 days. If not, Astral travel may need to be induced. Common techniques may be employed, though the most effective would be sensory deprivation or fixation.

If Astral travel is successful, the same methods may be extrapolated into use for contacting the spirits that will guide you through the maze surrounding the Throne. Refine the technique until similar, slightly less potent states may be achieved within minutes, or even seconds. Purging doubt and hesitation is a necessity. Do not try to quiet your mind. Instead, acknowledge the thoughts you experience and allow them to fade. No attachments, as they are not your own. You are simply experiencing them.

This is the first step to properly communicating with the Spirits of the Other Side.

GUIDES

The most potent guides that have made themselves known thusfar through the Work of our Coven are Lasa and Aftzaqesh. For the sake of this example, the rite will be explained using Aftzaqesh assuming the role of guide.

He can be invoked through two methods. The first being more simple and modern in format, the second more traditional in format. Perform either one depending upon your preference.

METHOD 1

Gather together loose incense of Palo Santo, Blackthorn, Acacia, Wormwood, and Sulfur on top of coals, or any similar method that is available to you that will maintain flame for a few minutes. Light the flame, and beseech Aftzaqesh, Keeper of the Gates and Master of the Crossroads, to join you, speak, and appear, in whatever words are most ernest to you. Visualize the Gate of Becoming in flame before you. Meditate on the spirit of Aftzaqesh wrenching open the Gate of Becoming. It may twist and change form. Allow it. So long as it holds open.

METHOD 2

Draw on the floor using chalk, blood, bone dust, or Palo Santo ash the Gate of Becoming. Place black candles at the three points of the triangle, and red candles at the three remaining points of the square, with incense of Acacia, Frankincense, and Cypress before the northern point of the square. In the center, draw your focus sigil using the same technique. The focus sigil may vary depending upon the intent of the ritual. In the case of using our Coven's methods and intents, the center sigil must be the Mark of the Averse as designated by the Coven, to be drawn in charred tobacco leaves, human ash or bone dust, and oil. Never use cigarettes for the tobacco. The additives dilute the spirit.

Once the seals are drawn, call the quarters in widdershins W - S - E - N, according to your personal elemental Daemons. Coven Daemons in respective order are Aftzaqesh, Tathos, Peretzeth, and Na'atzoth respectively. Sit in the center, light the candles and incense, and begin the ritual.

You will need an athame, a chalice, and two of a type of mallet, stick, or bone to be struck against the seals.

MOVEMENT 1: THE CHALICE

The Chalice is representative of your Self. Thus the first and most important step is a cleaning of the inside of the chalice. Meditation upon this concept and how it relates to the work is key. Be sure to wash with water any residue of previous works, then use any ceremonial washes or smokes to reseal as you would normal. Something that resonates with you and your Daemon. Partially fill with water.

While in the square, take the chalice, raise above your head, vibrate an A# μ, and acknowledge self as Chalice.

Slowly pour out the water. If you feel the need to verbally speak, recite the following.

"I am seeker and follower, devoted and lover. Thou cosmic moon,
ye light beyond the stars that coats the blackness of the unformed.
Hear me as I hear your words echoing within my heart. My soul
reflects your limitless light, and thus shall my mind become as

though your own. As this Chalice is emptied, so is my mind. So is my heart. So is my soul. I submit myself to your Will and open myself to your presence."

Vibrate G# α

Fill the Chalice with a fine red wine, bourbon, absinthe, or rum. Home made is best, but a favored brand of yours works as well.

"As this vessel before me is filled, so is this vessel of clay that I call my Self. Through this cup shall the spirit shall be born unto me, and through this vessel of I shall your spirit be born unto this world."

Drink, and offer the remaining to your Daemons in gratitude for their assistance.

MOVEMENT 2: THE ATHAME

Though many times I have heard Swords or Blades interpreted as Air, the blade is a weapon of war, and Martial energy. Even in utility, the blade is the manifestation of Azazel, and the very spirit of Qayin.

Lift the Athame and point towards the sky.

"Nemō Vāxsh! From blackened earth to starry sky, let the culmination of power passed through my ancestors be manifest in me. The heavenly thread of incarnations shall end with me! The Vulture descends!"

Slash downward at a right-to-left angle. Point the blade to the ground.

"Nemō Xshafua! From the heart of the eternal fire to the depths of the timeless ocean, let the collective will of the unconscious be manifest in me. The noose of Bhairava shall close upon me. The Scarab ascends!"

Slash downward at a left-to-right angle. Hold the blade pointed upward close to your chest. Feel the energy of the indwelling spirit that had transferred to you from the chalice transforming into a raging fire. Focus this energy upon the tip of the blade and vibrate F# η. Touch the tip to your Third Eye.

Response and following actions required may vary. Listen well and don't doubt.

MOVEMENT 3: THE EARTH

Saturn is associated with the alchemical element of Air. However, in Chinese mysticism, it is associated with Earth. This is much more appropriate for our Work in this context, as the vibratory frequency of the actual planet Saturn resonates in harmony with Earth, and is associated with Tau ת in Qabalah, which also represents the Earth element. In this sense, Saturn is the crossroads, the midway point between our Earthly abode and the underworld darkness represented in Pluto, and that which lies beyond our solar system. This is where most of the standard explanations and direction for the ritual break down, as this begins the inward journey. All work from here on is Astral in nature. Physical representations will change according to what happens within the liminal world.

Hold your hands over the fire of the candle, burning the hair and scorching the skin. The smell is pleasing to them. Scatter ashes, bone dust, blood, or sulfur. You may be asked by the spirit to coat parts of your body with it. At times when the spirits are especially hungry, or needing proof of devotion, self-flagellation or cutting to bleed upon the seals may be necessary. Once they are satisfied with your offerings, the trance begins. Often it is good to have something to draw/write with and on.

As you are coming out of the trance, take what mallets or bones you have and perform a simple beat on one or multiple points of the triangle. If you are using bone, do not stop until the bones break.

MOVEMENT 4: XEPER

Following the breaking of the bones or beating of the mallets, vibrate the formula "ZAZAS ZAZAS NASATANADA ZAZAS" 3 times, while tracing the sigil of Moloch - or any sigil that may have been transmitted to you during the trance - in the air with the athame, visualizing black fire maintaining the form. End and seal with a proclamation of "XEPERU"

In either method, a successful invocation should be met with an offering of 1 fruit, 1 flower, and 1 leaf or trimming from a plant commonly used in folk magic native to your area.

UPON COMPLETION OF THE RITUAL

Once the paths have been carved into the membrane of your causal reality, movement between the point will slowly become easier, and require less preparation. Meditation upon the concepts and sigils will certainly assist in this.

The end goal is to be able to open small portals in daily life, like planting seeds, as it were, but much more violently. To open the gateways between worlds and rend the veils of existence. The more these gateways are opened, the more powerful the Master's presence in this world, until the Words of Creation fall silent, and All is None.

The Gatekeeper's Seal

THE RITE OF HOLY POSSESSION

The following may be considered a sort of 'Lesser Ritual of Invocation' for usage in channeling the spirits of the Higher Order. More accurately, it is a call for willing Possession by the entity in question. By this means, the Will and Voice of the Spirit may be brought to engrave itself upon this world. This method has proven useful for presenting the essence of the spirits via Art and in Communication with others on this realm, thus allowing the Practitioner to be a mouthpiece and arm for the Spirit, for the sake of realization and manifestation of their Will upon this Earth.

You will need standard ritual tools such as a chalice, athame, and a ritual space that is at least 5sq ft (1.5sq m). You will also need incense of Aftzaqesh (1 part Tobacco, 2 parts Clove, and 1 part of a type of wood associated with the underworld, such as Cedar or Cypress) a drink of his favor (old-recipe beer, ale, bourbon, or mead), and at least one item that is associated to the Higher Order Spirit which you are attempting to contact (said item either being listed in the Codex, or discerned from your own personal Work). The more associated items the better, as at least one must be burned as part of the rite, and the others may be used as psychospiritual anchors for the entity and practitioner alike, allowing for an easier bridging of the not-so-proverbial gap.

If invoking Na'atzoth, or Zathane, be sure to include Palo Santo wood or incense (or add 1 part Rose, Palo Santo, or Blackthorn to Aftzaqesh's incense), dirt from a crossroads, and a cutting of a thorned plant as an offering to Lasa as the Keeper of the Way for the two.

To begin, draw on the ground the Gate of Becoming, with the Pictographic Seal of Aftzaqesh in the center. As you are seated in the center of the Gate -on top of the central Seal- place around you as many of the associated items (plants, spices, stones or metals, totems, and fetishes, etc.) of the Higher Order Spirit you are attempting to contact as feasible for your situation and environment.

Call the quarters in your own inspired or directed manner in widdershins order, ending with the cardinal direction associated with said Higher Order Spirit.

Face the cardinal direction associated with the Higher Order Spirit and light the incense of Aftzaqesh. Offer to Him the liquid sacrifice with a request of favor in your endeavors.

> "Great keeper of the Gates, Lord of Crossed Roads, Great Father of Ten Thousand Names, I come before you as one devoted to the darkest Will of our Lord, humbly, and bearing _______ as offering, crafted in the ways of old. May it please you, that you may look favorably upon my request. I entreat you, reach forth from beyond and grasp tightly upon this seal, and wrench open for me the Way to your Kingdom, that I might commune with the One"

If invoking Na'atzoth, or Zathane, mirror this verbal request with a similar entreatment of Lasa.

At this point, call the Higher Order Spirit you are attempting to commune with. At least one offering should be of a manner that can be burned. As part of the invocation, you must burn the offering to ashes, and smear the ashes on your forehead.

"Through the Gate that was opened for me, I call your name, _______. Through the Way that was prepared for me, I call to you, ________. As a favored child of Darkness and Death, my soul branded with the mark of your Will, I come before you. I present to you this offering of _______, may the scent of its burning be pleasing to you, that you would hear well my request with sincerity."

Light the offering, meditate upon the image, concepts, and forms of the spirit as offering burns.

"Let my mind be a door through which you enter. Let my body be a vehicle through which you move. Let my spirit be unified with yours. May the song of my essence resonate with your own. May this vessel be filled with your presence. I cast out all thought and energy that is not of your Being. There is no other here but you."

Once it is completely burnt, take ash from the offering and smear it on your brow or face.

Conduct your intended duties while visualizing sigils of the spirit, or while staring at printed/drawn sigil of the spirit, making sure to keep the ash on your brow.

When your work is completed, bow and meditate at the altar, thank the spirit for its assistance. Snuff out any candles, but leave any remaining offering on the altar, and leave any incense burning to completion. Clean yourself of ash a debri, but do not make an attempt to close the gate. Instead, simply clean the ritual area as necessary for daily appearances and practical use.

SEAL OF THE AVERSE NAME

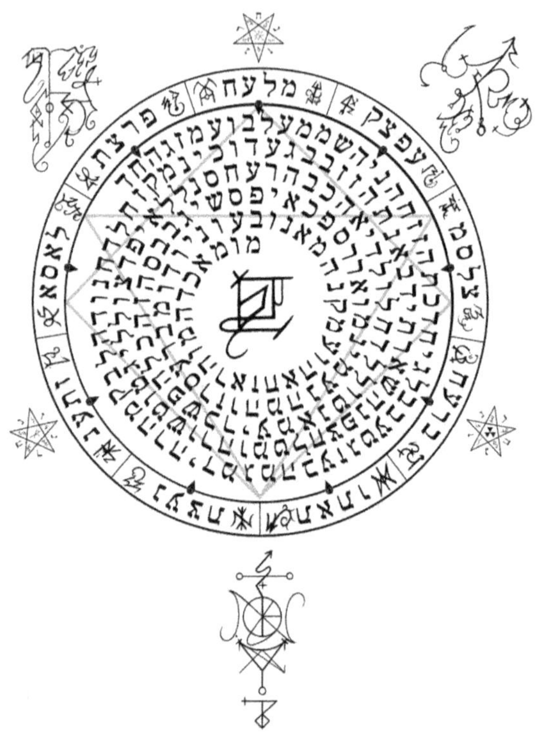

The culmination of all formulas present in this text can be distilled
into a singular sigil, which we call the Seal of the Averse Name. The
sigil was fashioned with part willful intent to create an effective gateway, and part automatic writing in trance. Gematria calculations and
personal ritual experience have molded the seal and its parts to facilitate invocation of the Nameless Averse as practitioners of the Inner
Temple have experienced it in the past. As more have utilized this
seal, and those established continue to delve further into the intrica-
cies and nuance of the patterns and letters, it becomes more potent.
The sigils on the corners as well as the top and bottom points work in

unison to enhance the process of possession by the spirit or power, calling upon specific aspects of practitioner psyche and daemonic axioms to strip ego and facilitate indwelling communication. The meaning of each piece will be explained in this section in detail, though not in full, as the implications are far-reaching, and are continually revealing themselves.

The key for effective use is not to push your way into it, but to allow it to rise up through you. You're not calling anything, it is calling you.

The center lettering of the circle, and surrounding ring, is composed of Hebrew lettering correlating with Greek, Avestan, and Sanskrit, translating for the most part gibberish if just read in Hebrew with no context. The script of Hebrew -or more accurately, Aramaic- was used as a means of connecting this work with established currents and majority bias of Readers, that this system and method may be seen for what it is - a vehicle for thought divergent from existing systems. That which is presented here is done so in a manner suited for introduction and initiation unto the system of the Chapel of Vedantic Nihilism. The use of familiar terms and characters is nothing more than a guiding sign for further development beyond that which has been established. The Daemons of this Star and Seal exist to bring the practitioner to a new level of paradoxal and chaotic understanding. One cannot pass through the gates to the underworld without first knowing their location, and discerning the path to the threshold is the first necessary step to its crossing.

The 216-letter name encircling the central character may be split into segments of 3, mirroring the 72-letter name of Elohim, and the 72 Demons of the Goetia, which we know are representative of mental processes and thus, Daemons. Noospheric entities as described in the beginning of this document. They are not exclusively the given lettering or concept, but a numeric, gematria-based segmented formula. The 72 constellations of 3 letters may be grouped and considered in a similar manner. However, in meditating upon these powers, the practitioner should never be so foolish as to limit the scope of their understanding of these entities. They are Noospheric in nature, and thus they may be objective, subjective, or metapersonal. They are a wisp of Nothing upon the tides of infinity. Their purpose is to Negate the original and opposing 72, and thus exist to balance and nullify the Goetia and the hosts of Heaven. This may sometimes require violent psychological intervention.

The 72 Daemons may each be further grouped into segments of 8, creating 9 individual greater, or higher entities. Daemon Rulers. Primary aspects and emanations, masks of the Nameless King. Like 9 separate personalities at congress within the psychotic mind of a god on the threshold of the Abyss. The gematria total of this name is 12,626, equalling 8 - the number of cosmic infinity, the hebrew letter Cheth. This denotes the nature of reality in duality, and division. In the knowledge of construction, we receive equal knowledge of deconstruction. The keys to immortality unlock as well the gates of Death. Hesperus is Phosphorus.

The nature and influence of the 9 are further explored lyrically and magickally in Grave Gnosis' works.

THE NAMES of the 9 on the outer circle in Widdershins order are:

Moloch - the King of Fire
Peretzeth - the Queen of Desire
Lasa - the Serpent of the Crossroads
Zathane - the Maw of Time
Na'atzoth - the Fury of Karma
Tathos - the Voice of the Master
Berachesh - the Raven-Saint
Tzelsamon - the Shadow of the Lord
Aftzaqesh - the Keeper of the Gate

THE 9 ARE aspects of the One, but manifest as separate intelligences that may be invoked as one would any Daemon. They have associations to stars, planets, metals, plants, animals, and elements, and thus may be invoked and evoked according to varying traditions and systems of Magick. The materials and associations will be noted in the following section. They may be referred to in future sections as the Higher Order of Spirits. Their names were divined through a mix of gematria and trance inspiration. They do refer to each other, and may skip the final syllable of the names. In specific reference: Aftzaqesh is often called Aftzaq, and Tzelsamon called Tzelsam.

ON THE ORDERING OF THE NINE

There are two orders of procession through the 9, each forming a separate design. The first order follows a similar pattern to the traditional 'Tree of Life' design, and aligns the spirits to their Qabalistic and Qliphotic counterparts' locations. The first order listed here from the bottom of the tree to the top (following lightning-bolt formation upward, minus the equivalent of Malkuth) is as follows:

Aftzaqesh
Tzelsamon
Berachesh
Tathos
Na'atzoth
Zathane
Lasa
Peretzeth
Moloch

THIS IS the Path of Pestilence Crowned. This version of the Path is much more suited to introductory levels of work, and for those who are transitioning from Christianity or Atheism, or who have started their Occult studies with the archetypal system of Qabalah. It is designed to be a direct link between concepts of both orthodox Qabalah and the heretical Qliphoth, and nullify them.

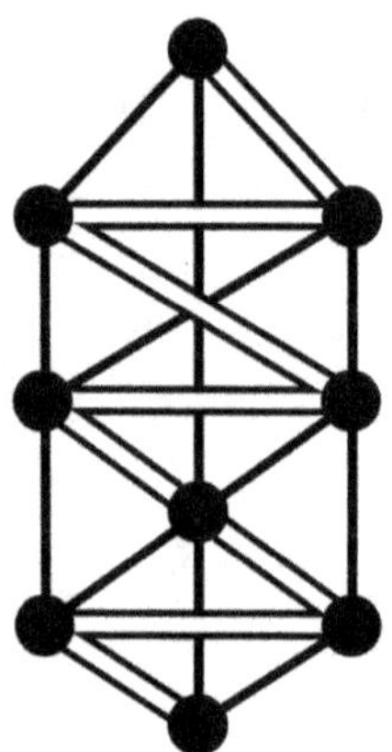

The second order is more aligned to the actual procession of the spiritual aspects as you would encounter them naturally on your journey, or in a full, grand rite and meditation. This also mirrors the order in which they revealed themselves to the Coven. The second order listed here from the bottom seat to the highest is as follows:

Aftzaqesh

Na'atzoth

Zathane

Berachesh

Lasa

Peretzeth

Tathos

Tzelsamon

Moloch

This is the Path of the Lux Nigredo, designed in a way that focuses on practical application and study, compounding upon itself in procession to Moloch's throne. This is the Path of true Devotion to the Nameless King of the Void. There may be many alternative interpretations of the pathways and the figure itself, as it shifts upon the streams of consciousness according to the perspective of the individual practitioner, but we have here a sigilic figure that most accurately represents Moloch pathworking as it has been presented within our Temple. The Crossroads, the pillars of the Temple, the Key and the Gate, the Sun, the Shadow, and the Infinite Flames. This order also portrays the pairings and associations much more appropriately, and in an almost mythic fashion, beginning at the Crossroads of Nod, governed by Lasa, connecting Berachesh, Zathane, Na'atzoth, and Aftzaqesh. By their joining, we reach the Thrones of the King and Queen of the Nous in Tathos and Peretzeth. Finally, we are consumed by the Flames That Cast Not Light, But Shadow, in the powers of Tzelsamon and Moloch. Thus beholding the face of Death and the body of Choronzon.

The Reader should note that Aftzaqesh and Moloch stand in the same place for both orderings.

THE HIGHER ORDER OF SPIRITS

ZATHANE

Syncretic Associations:
Za'afiel, Baal Hamon, Neith, Anat

24-Character Name:
התנאבדיתראשהנפצחלטמזהרוש

Legions:
Hayanchemer - ܡܐܐܢܫܒܝ

Gematria et Lux Magia:
Jupiter - Fire/Water
Tin
315 - 9
Prime Aspect - 527
Lesser Spirits - 2203
C# Diminished
4/4
Purple & Red

Other Gematriatic Associations:
Father's Seat, Morh - the cave, Gomorrah, Gihon - the second river,
Thirst of Time, the Great Span of Separation, Trickster, gathered
legions

The Maw of Time

THE BRAZEN-FACED INCARNATION of indiscriminate punishment. All life is sin, all thoughts and deeds are criminal. The righteous seeking ascension are greeted by the gaping maw of Kala. They weep in horror and the shock of realization.

Subversive and sinister in her rule, a manifestation of Chaos. Taking pleasure in its own foolishness and unfettered bloodlust. A great flood of primordial waters, promulgating conflict as a virus.

Presence of this entity and its works may lead to odd passages of time, with possession sometimes manifesting as missing time. Facilitates movement through this dual reality, and such situations where duality may confound. May bring success, but may humble at a moment's notice if pride is found, or ownership of the success is claimed by the invoker. Will certainly attempt to trick the practitioner into failure as much as she does assist, for growth is only found in conflict. Her greatest lesson is to outwit the trickster, refuse to play the game, and win the war without ever fighting a battle.

One of the few overtly Feminine spirits, though androgynous in its nature, taking what our society would consider masculine names, titles, and faces. A sly warrior queen most often associated with War and Victory.

Jackal or Coyote bone pendants and fetishes will allow for a maintained presence. Goat and Ram hides or horns, and peacock feathers are accepted as offerings.

SIGILS

Psychological Manifestations

Discipline, adaptability, conflict resolution, objective stances in arguments, or inciting conflict in others

Conscious	Magick Squares	Subconscious	Unconscious
		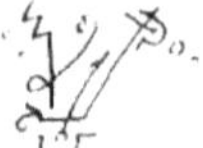	

Spiritual Manifestation

Invocation	Evocation	via Mercury	via Venus
	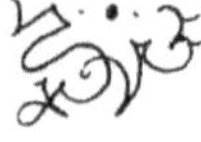		

Prime Sigils

Traditional (Magick Square)   Inspired (Channeled)

Pictographic Representation

www.ingramcontent.com/pod-product-compliance
Lightning Source LLC
Chambersburg PA
CBHW070842160726

48004CB00001B/465